HUNT
FOR THE
TROLL

HUNT
FOR THE
TROLL

MARK RICHARDSON

THE NEW ATLANTIAN LIBRARY
is an imprint of
ABSOLUTELY AMAZING eBOOKS

Published by Whiz Bang LLC, 926 Truman Avenue, Key West, Florida 33040, USA.

For information contact:
Publisher@AbsolutelyAmazingEbooks.com

ISBN-13: 978-0692518700 (New Pulp Press)
ISBN-10: 0692518703

For my mother,
an amazing woman

"In the universe, there are things that are known, and things that are unknown, and in between, there are doors."

- William Blake

HUNT
FOR THE
TROLL

PART I

When the Troll first appeared in my mind's eye, I thought it was a dream.

This seemed a logical conclusion because I was asleep. Of course, logic and dreams don't necessarily mesh. A dream world has its own rules, and logic is rarely a part of it.

Typically my dreams are very dreamlike, and by that I mean not very realistic. For example, a woman will be riding an elephant, and then I'll be naked, and she'll start chasing me, and although I can barely move my feet, she can't catch me – that sort of thing. But this seemed so genuine.

A Troll – *what the hell?*

But before the Troll appeared, there was darkness: a black hole, a door slammed on solitary confinement. I was effectively blind.

Then light. Just a little illumination, but it grew, as if someone were slowly lifting a dimmer switch. It was a warm, comforting, electrifying glow, like the end of a perfect summer day. I was inside a room: enormous, infinite. It was as vast as space itself. Like space, gravity didn't apply, so I floated. My body was enveloped by soothing and titillating warmth.

I belong here, I thought.

In time I saw a door float past. Soon many doors materialized. They were all closed, and on the front of each one was a series of numbers, zeroes and ones: 100101, for example – binary code.

As I mulled over their meaning, the Troll appeared. He'd flown out of one of the floating doors, his face etched with a determined scowl.

My brain struggled to make sense of the strange scene when another door appeared. With one enormous hand, the Troll pushed that one open and slipped inside. The door slammed shut, and I could see that sketched just below the frame, in big black numbers, was the code 00101010. Briefly I wondered where that door led, when far in the distance I saw the Troll step through another door. He moved effortlessly out of it and toward another, opened that one and entered. Soon, all around me – near and a great distance away – more doors appeared. There were too many to count. Maybe there were thousands, or perhaps millions. With splendid alacrity, he glided from one door to the next, appeared and then disappeared again. My sense was that the Troll himself had willed them to appear.

I hovered and watched, slack-jawed.

As I watched, the doors changed. The binary code vanished and was replaced with circles, 3-D spheres. These spheres were bisected with both vertical and horizontal axis. There were numbers as well, lots of them, and complex mathematical equations. The numbers seemed to change their denomination depending on how I looked at them. I'd never seen anything like it.

It was beautiful.

The Troll kept flying through the doors, picking up speed, moving like a thought firing through brain synapses. At no point did I consider following him. I'm not even sure if I could have. My role was that of a spectator. He started to move even faster, zipped from one door to the next, became a blur, a shooting star, a flicker of light.

Then the Troll floated through the door that was nearest to me.

"Nice to meet you," I said. The Troll rubbed his bulky and big chin. He shared a fleeting resemblance to Rodin's Thinker, muscular, contemplative. "You're amazingly lifelike for a dream. In fact, all of this," I waved my hand toward the vast sea of doors, "looks very realistic."

"This isn't a dream."

"What?"

"We're inside the Internet, the cloud. We're networked through your neural processor."

He was right, I realized, I wasn't dreaming, as I've told you. But the weird thing was that I was still asleep, and in my sleeping state, I was having an actual dream at the same time that I spoke with the Troll. With a little effort, I could jump between realities, kind of like using a TV remote controller. And while I jumped between those worlds, it felt like there was a third reality – the real me, let's call it – perched above it all, observing. It was trippy.

We're networked through your neural processor?

But that wasn't possible. Or was it? "How's that possible?" I asked.

The Troll smiled. He studied my face. One second, two seconds – time shuffled forward. Eventually he said, cryptically, "We're going to change the world."

Then the Troll did a backstroke away from where I hovered. He moved lightly and with surprising grace for someone so large. Watching him go was awesome and a little comical. He drifted through a door and everything vanished.

≈≈≈

What's funny is that I didn't wake up. Instead, I continued to sleep until the sun shone through my bay window and jolted me awake. Magnus Carlsen rubbed his head against my chin and meowed for his breakfast.

"I'll get to you in a second, little buddy."

I sat up in bed. With my fingertips, I rubbed the back

3

of my head, where the neural processor had been installed.

Did that really happen? Had I really been visited by a Troll?

Yeah, I had, I decided.

My next thought was*: What the fuck?* More thoughts flowed in rapid succession: *That was cool. Who is the Troll? How can I find him again?*

My head was spinning and I hadn't even had a first cup of coffee.

Instinctually, I grabbed my iPhone off the bedside table and checked to see if I had any new messages: email, text, voice.

Nada.

I stretched, swung my legs off the bed, slipped my feet into my slippers, found my robe, and walked the few steps to my tiny kitchen. There I brewed a pot of coffee and dished out a plate of tuna fish and a bowl of milk for Magnus. He meowed a thank you before diving in.

I polished off a cup of joe. Questions continued to percolate through my head. But I didn't have time to fully work my way to any answers, if landing on answers was even a realistic possibility. I mean, a Troll visited me in the middle of the night.

A Troll, really?

Anyway, I'd been tipped off that a group of Orcs had conducted a massive invasion during the night. The destruction would be substantial, and I imagined that I had a full day of sweeping ahead of me.

I needed to dash off to work. There wasn't even time to shower.

2

You're probably familiar with my life story, or more accurately, the Silicon Valley archetype, which is what my life roughly resembled. In middle school I became enamored with computers and positively obsessed with writing software. In high school I started selling programs to large companies on the Peninsula, things like security tools, social networking apps, what have you. As a result, during my senior year I earned more money than both of my parents. People began to tout my programming prowess, tossing around words like "prodigy" and "genius."

I was given a full scholarship at Stanford. It was during my very first semester that I met the Captain.

Now, some of the best programmers in history have been saddled with the nickname "Captain Crunch." Unfortunately, this Captain wasn't one of them. He was little better than a weekend hacker, a hobbyist.

Late one night, a week or so after Halloween, I showed him a data mining application that I'd been developing.

"What exactly is this supposed to do?" he asked, in my dorm room, between sips from a bottle of Heineken.

"It tracks how people use the Internet, what sites they visit, what they buy – that sort of thing. It's called audience measurement technology."

"Really? It sounds a little Big Brotherish."

"Yeah, I suppose. It would allow companies to customize their advertisements for each online visitor."

The Captain's eyelids fluttered as if he was working to

calculate a complex math equation. "We're going to use this to start a company," he said, flashing me a gap-toothed smile. "You're a genius, you know that, the new Edison."

Before Thanksgiving we dropped out of school and launched our company. We called it Polpo, the word for octopus in Italian. We liked the thought of our tentacles reaching out and pulling things back – primarily money.

Maybe you're now expecting to hear how our start-up caught fire, how the Captain and I became billionaires, like the founders at Twitter and Google and Facebook, to name just a few? That was the goal – definitely – and it was pursued with a single-minded focus. But it wasn't in the cards. Despite the fact that for three years all I did, all I thought about, all I dreamed about was how to make Polpo a success, the Captain and I could never find a way to differentiate ourselves from a growing field of competitors. So after some hand-wringing, we eventually accepted our fate, sold off the technology to Google, and went our separate ways.

≈≈≈

Through the sale of Polpo, I made enough money so that I didn't need to work, at least not for a good while. So I decamped to Rome. My plan was to spend a month there before branching out to the rest of the country, the grand Italian tour. But Rome suited me. So much so that after just a few days, I decided to settle down and rented a tiny studio near Campo de Fiori. I didn't speak the language, not well anyway, although I had started to learn it. Besides, most Italians knew at least a smattering of English, usually much more. I made a handful of friends, enough that for essentially the first time in memory I had a budding social life. I went to parties and sporting events and enjoyed taking long walks. I was enamored with the city's architecture, the oldness and muted colors. For hours I'd wander aimlessly, exploring, soaking in the sights. Or spend an entire morning at a café drinking espressos and studying old chess games.

Anyway, one carefree month followed another. How many months? I'm not certain. Moreover, time, as Einstein pointed out, is not a constant. Perhaps during that period in Rome time moved at a slower pace than what I'd grown accustomed to? Or at least it's fun to think so.

So I loafed. I was happy. Life was good.

Life was so good, in fact, that I made a decision to live in Rome permanently. Why not? There was nothing to tie me to my old existence. I could reinvent myself and create an Italian iteration, a version dedicated to pursuing life's simple pleasures.

But then I received an email and those dreams were pushed aside.

It came from the Captain. The note rambled, but its essence was that he'd uncovered a new business opportunity, planned to launch another company, wanted me to join him.

Dude, I need you, he wrote.

I bought a plane ticket home immediately. I didn't reason out the decision. It was made with my gut. But if I had pushed beyond my gut and examined my thoughts, deep down, I wanted to get back in the tech start-up game.

But when I arrived in the Bay Area, the Captain was nowhere to be found. His cell didn't work. Or his email account. Through the manager of his apartment building, I learned that the Captain hadn't paid his rent. I searched and searched, but couldn't find him. He'd vanished. I felt lost.

Momentarily, I considered going back to Rome, but dropped that idea quickly. It felt like I'd abandoned that path. And then, out of the blue, I was offered a job at an online gaming company called Centre Terrain. I took it. I rented a one-bedroom apartment in San Francisco on top of Nob Hill. I'd lived there for eighteen months when the Troll made that dreamy nighttime visit.

3

The first day after the visit from the Troll, I walked to work. It was a thirty-minute trip from my apartment, door-to-door. I didn't own a car, and although I could have ridden the bus, or, God forbid, a cable car, I always walked, rain or shine.

That particular day the weather was perfect. The air crisp – jacket temp – but also sunny: the sky as blue as a new marble. It was the last Friday in September, which is dependably the best weather month in San Francisco. After a fog-filled summer, there'd been a month's worth of sunshine.

As I left Nob Hill and descended California Street, I called my friend Whitfield.

He answered after the third ring. "Keemo." His voice was scratchy, a smoker's rasp.

"Are you free tonight?" I asked, skipping the pleasantries.

My mind raced with thoughts of the Troll. I could still feel the warm sensation of affinity that had hit me the previous night. *We're going to change the world*, he'd said.

I wanted to get Whitfield's take. He was as well connected as it gets in the Valley. If there was anyone who knew about the Troll, I figured, it would be him. Besides, he was my bud, and I wanted to see him.

"I was hoping I could swing by." I had to practically yell so that I could be heard over the clanging bell of an ascending cable car.

"Yeah." He coughed, cleared his throat. "What time?"

"Sixish?"

"I'll see you then."

≈≈≈

After exactly a half-hour, I arrived at Centre Terrain's headquarters, which was housed in a cool (some might call it "handsome") redbrick mid-rise on Howard Street, at the edge of the Financial District, just a block from the Embarcadero. The building was a landmark. It was originally built by The Folgers Coffee Company, way back around the time of that firm's founding in 1850, an era when San Francisco was focused on gold, not technology. I knew this because there was a bronzed historical plaque on the wall at the front entrance.

I pushed through the revolving doors and into the lobby, gave a nod to the fat, donut-eating security guard, and rode up the elevator. It sped past the second floor (administration), the third (marketing), the fourth (management), and eased to a stop on the fifth floor. That's where the Sweepers kept shop. I was a Sweeper, another name for a programmer charged with fixing flaws in the Centre Terrain program.

I had a reputation for arriving to work late, but I glanced at a clock and saw it was 9:28, meaning that I still had twelve minutes until the start of the morning team meeting. Still not fully caffeinated, I made a beeline for the coffee room, where I found Nika preparing a cup. She'd apparently just finished tearing the lids off those little plastic containers that hold cream. There was a sticky pile of empty containers on the counter in front of her.

"That's a lot of creamers," I said, making a quick tally.

"I always use seven."

"Really, why's that?"

"Eight is one too many and six just ain't enough." She frowned, annoyed, and seemed to imply that I should mind my own business, but after just a couple of beats that irritated expression melted away and she asked me, "Pleasant dreams?"

It struck me as an odd question for a couple reasons. First, my visit from the Troll the previous night had been particularly unusual and vivid. Second, Nika had never before made a point of engaging me in a conversation. Actually, the opposite was true: she seemed to go out of her way to avoid me. The conversation about the creamers ranked up there as one of the longest we'd ever had.

"Just your standard stuff," I said, "a spinning hamster wheel." This actually had been a recurring dream of mine: me, racing on an enormous hamster wheel, running faster and faster until I woke up in a clammy sweat.

"I see." She stirred her coffee with a tiny straw. "You don't need Freud to decipher that one."

"I suppose not," I said.

What Nika said next floored me.

"Hey, I've been meaning to ask you. Would you be up for grabbing a bite to eat? Dinner, I mean. I know a really good Italian place in North Beach. The gnocchi there is *amazing.*"

In total, Centre Terrain employed fifty-four Sweepers, and Nika was one of only seven women. All the Sweepers worked on rotating six-hour shifts, ensuring that there was never a time that the network wasn't properly monitored. Nika and I were assigned to the same time frame, weekdays 10:00 a.m. to 4:00 p.m. This was a peak time for the game, when the network was under the most potential strain, and Nika was selected for it because she was an amazing programmer; although, frankly, she wasn't up to my level. No one was. That's not arrogance or bragging. It was the unavoidable truth.

As for her appearance, depending on your perspective, she was either homely or one of those women who leapt over cute and landed squarely on beautiful. Her nose wasn't in proportion, but was just a tad out of whack. She wore black eyeliner mascara below her eyes, applied widely enough so that it brought to mind a raccoon. On her left eyebrow, there was a little gold, arrow-shaped piercing. Her hair was dyed lollipop-red, and was so bright it strained the eyes to look at. Still, you couldn't look away because something about her pulled you in. She kept her hair long, shoulder length, in part, I believed, to the cover up the fact that she was missing an ear. That's right, in the spot where her right ear should have resided it was just skin, as smooth as the skin on her cheek. No one ever discussed the abnormality, but I assumed it was the result of a bizarre birth defect.

For clothes, Nika opted for the grunge look. That day in the coffee room she wore a man's baggy flannel shirt, an equally baggy pair of black jeans, and ankle-high Dr. Martens boots.

Now when it came to assessing Nika's appearance, I fell squarely into the "beautiful" camp. Despite the fact that her oversized clothes made it nearly impossible to accurately judge her body, I sensed she was hiding something rather spectacular. And she emitted an unmistakable erotic energy. On a couple of occasions, the force of that energy had hit me with such potency that, seeking relief, after work I'd squirreled myself away in the handicapped bathroom and jacked off into a wad of paper towels.

"Dinner," I responded to her invitation, trying to keep my cool. "Yeah, that sounds like fun. When did you have in mind?"

"How 'bout tonight?"

I almost said yes, but remembered that I'd made plans with Whitfield. "Could we do it tomorrow instead?" I asked, fully planning to change my plans if she couldn't make it.

"That works." She gave me a playful smile that caused my skin to prickle with goose bumps. She told me the name of the restaurant, and we confirmed that we'd meet the next night at seven. We exchanged cell phone numbers and then walked together to our staff meeting.

≈≈≈

We arrived at 9:40 a.m. on the button. The other Sweepers were already seated at their workstations, and Edzard, our manager, stood in front of them at a mobile whiteboard. He used a black marker to jot down some statistics.

"As anticipated, last night was one of the busiest of the year."

With his pen, he wrote: *400,000 individual visitors.*

"All that traffic kept the Sweepers busy."

He wrote: *75 tears in the network.*

A tear was a colloquial term for a programming bug. Centre Terrain was extraordinarily complex, with more than ten billion lines of code, so large it was almost like a living organism. Bugs constantly cropped up. Because of the game's complexity, a Sweeper had to be inside the game to accurately identify a bug. Once one was discovered, a Sweeper activated a dialogue box inside the game (a pop-up window) and wrote code that corrected the issue before a problem became severe. Sometimes it was a race against time, a definite adrenaline rush. I dug it.

Edzard continued. "But those tears were minor and all were immediately fixed by your predecessors. As a result, we experienced no network downtime."

He wrote "zero" on the board and underlined it.

"I expect nothing less from all of you. Now, as you know, the North American gamers are about to go online, which means we'll likely double that 400,000 number from last night. So I need you all to..."

I tuned him out. The rest was Edzard's standard pre-game motivational speech, which I'd heard hundreds of times. So I settled into my seat, tried to get centered, and scanned my surroundings.

The Sweepers' fifth-floor aerie was one giant room. Scattered throughout were a dozen tables. Each Sweeper was equipped with the latest Mac Pro, tweaked for maximum performance and souped-up with the company's own customized software. Near one wall stood a pool table, which was practically never used, and two bean bag chairs. Toward the kitchen was a life-sized cutout of Mr. Spock. The walls were brick, the pipes exposed. Square windows were sprinkled throughout the room, windows that actually opened.

"All right," said Edzard, in a voice loud enough that it snapped me back to attention. "It's game time. T-minus three, two, one..."

I slipped on my glasses and morphed into Roma; the world materialized around him, and he was inside.

≈≈≈

The name Centre Terrain, as you may have surmised, is a blatant rip-off of Middle Earth from *The Lord of the Rings*. I was told that the company's founders had hired a marketing firm that charged a criminally large amount of money to dream up a catchy name, but after weeks of deliberations and a dozen focus groups, "Centre Terrain" was the best they could come up with. The game featured Orcs and elves and dragons and other exotic creatures. Players – gamers – each had their own avatar. But what set Centre Terrain apart from the other multitudes of games out there was the quality of its graphical environment. To login, users wore augmented reality glasses, which made it possible for an imaginary world to form around them. The sensation was spectacular. Once inside, you literally felt like you'd entered a real world. I'll tell you, if you were to examine an actual rose, and then one created in Centre Terrain, you'd be unable to tell the difference, except the computer-generate rose would seem more authentic.

Each Sweeper also had an avatar. Mine was named Roma: a human warrior with a physique that brought to mind Thor, although Roma was darker, more brooding. He had a wide scar that ran from his right temple down to his chin. One tooth was missing – a lateral incisor – and he sported a permanent five o'clock shadow. He was a badass.

The Sweepers' avatars were God-like. Although technically confined by the rules of the game, they could transport themselves to any level instantaneously, explore the virtual world at light speed. There were no opponents who could legitimately challenge them. Sometimes a Sweeper would run across a testosterone-fueled thug who'd attack and immediately get slaughtered. But most encounters with gamers were friendly, if not downright obsequious.

≈≈≈

Roma scoured the game's first level for bugs, found none, and worked his way upward, tackling each subsequent rank one at a time. He repaired minor tears on levels four and eight, and a fairly large one – a rupture that had the potential to bring down the entire network – on number thirteen. He spent nearly an hour writing code to fix it.

With that behind him, Roma decided to kick back, do some exploring. Although such activity wasn't approved by company management, Roma had made a habit of it. He liked to uncover new areas in the game, areas designed and built by third-party developers.

Roma landed in a tiny village. It was populated with

Halflings, another Middle Earth rip-off. As he strode down a street, Roma was mobbed by a friendly horde of little people. They patted him on the back. They asked if they could buy him a beer at the pub, an offer that Roma readily accepted.

The pub was cozy. It had a low ceiling, a wooden interior. There was a large rectangular bar in the middle. A fireplace nearly filled up an entire wall. The room buzzed with conversation. Roma sat at the bar and polished off three pints of brew. As he considered ordering another, he noticed something peculiar: all of the Halflings were women. That was more than a little unusual because most gamers were men, and although some men had female avatars, research had shown that most people stuck with their real-life gender.

Then it dawned on Roma: he'd stumbled onto a lesbian enclave. There'd been an article about such developments in one of the trade rags that was dedicated to covering news related to Centre Terrain. When the game was first created, it was expected that people would join strictly for the warring aspects. But that didn't turn out to be the case. A lot of people signed-up with little or no interest in fighting at all, and lesbian communities, interestingly, had become commonplace. The article said that there was some editorial debate as to whether these societies were formed by actual lesbians seeking to create a utopia of sorts where same-sex marriage was legal, or by young men eager to live out their porn-inspired girl-on-girl fantasies. Either way, Roma approved of the development.

Roma went ahead and ordered another pint. But before the glass hit his lips, a low rumble, like a boulder rolling down a hill, came from outside the pub. The rumble grew louder. Soon it was a deafening roar. The Halflings raced out the pub's door into the bright sunshine and Roma followed. Together they were confronted by the awesome sight of an army of Orcs storming down the surrounding hills. The Orcs were clothed in full battle regalia – armor, shields, battle axes, even crossbows. They looked like an endless swarm of angry hornets. Roma did a quick census and estimated that the Halflings were outnumbered two-to-one, if not worse. If that weren't bad enough, Halflings weren't really designed to be warriors. It might take two or more to kill one Orc.

Roma scaled the pub's wall and sat on the roof, leaned against the chimney. He wanted to get a bird's eye view of the oncoming slaughter. What else could he do? His hands were tied. There was one unbreakable rule for each Sweeper: don't interfere. They were sent into Centre Terrain to make sure the program ran properly, nothing more. It was a hard-and-fast rule, one he'd never seen broken, not flagrantly anyway.

The Halflings pulled their swords, lifted their shields, braced for the onslaught, and as they did a sound cut through the Orc's feverish battle cries.

Baroom!

It caused the Orc horde to slow its descent, but they kept moving. Then the noise came again, only louder.

BAROOM!

It was earsplitting. The piercing loudness of the sound stopped both the Orcs and Halflings cold. Roma scanned the horizon and found where it originated, in a small strip of land that separated the two armies. There stood Jett. In one hand she held an enormous horn. She put her lips to its nozzle and blew: *BAROOM!* The virtual earth shook.

Jett was Nika's avatar, an elf with big pointy ears that Roma assumed she'd created to compensate for Nika's appendage deficiency. Jett gave off a similar vibe to the real-life Nika, funky and alternative. But whereas Nika's clothes were modest, Jett's outfit was provocative. Dressed completely in black leather, she was adorned with thigh-high platform boots, a skirt that just barely reached below her crotch, and a bikini-style bra top that tightly held her full, gravity-mocking breasts. Around her forehead she wore a thin headband. She looked like an impossibly sexy dominatrix.

Jett's sudden appearance stunned everyone, Roma included. There was a pregnant pause as all eyes turned toward her. This lasted just a couple of seconds, until Jett pulled her double-bladed sword from its scabbard, spun it over her head a few times, and moved into the sea of Orcs, where she proceeded to cut them down. In no time it was a bloody mess.

The Halflings, once they realized what was happening, let out a cheerful cry. The Orc horde, acting as a single entity, descended onto Jett. It didn't matter. The poor bastards didn't have a chance. The battle – if you want to call it that – lasted only fifteen minutes. In the end not one Orc survived.

When it was finished, the Halflings lifted Jett up onto their tiny shoulders and carried her into the pub. Just before entering the door, Jett looked upward at Roma, still perched on the pub's roof, and winked.

A moment later Roma heard a soft whimpering noise coming from behind. He turned his head and saw a Halfling, obviously a male, who stood just a foot or so from where Roma sat. The Halfling was shorter than normal, so short that his pant legs dragged on the ground. He had black hair, neatly cut, but his appearance was defined by his eyes, eyes so large they seemed to fill his entire face: sad, droopy, puppy dog eyes.

As Roma looked at him, the Halfling made the same whimpering noise again. It was soft and sounded like, "*Hmmmaaa...*"

Roma said, "Hey there," and sped away.

≈ ≈ ≈

The rest of the shift was uneventful. Roma uncovered a few more tears but nothing significant. He cleaned them up, did a few more rounds on levels eighteen through twenty-four, and prepared to log out for the day.

At exactly 4:00 p.m. I was kicked out of Centre Terrain. I rubbed my eyes, shook the cobwebs out of my head, and eased back into the real world. The sun had dipped and shone directly through the westward windows, illuminating the dust motes in the air, which gave the room a dreamy quality. It took me a moment to register that Edzard was standing just a few feet away, positioned exactly halfway between where Nika and I sat.

"You two – come with me," he said, his eyes squarely on Nika. His gaze was so intent that it seemed he would bore a hole in her skull.

We all walked to his office.

"You first," he said, and glanced my way, before swiveling his gaze back to Nika. "You – outside," he grunted, "I'll get to you later."

Edzard's office was the only one on the fifth floor. It was tucked away in a corner, tiny and windowless. Edzard was apparently a hoarder because the room was cluttered with books and trade show tchotchkes. Unruly stacks of paper were piled on his desk. It was beyond cramped.

"Sit," he said. I had to clear space on the chair by removing two binders, which I deposited on the floor, and sat on the employee side of the desk. Edzard sat down as well, on his chair. He leaned back. "I wanted to remind you about Monday," he said.

Monday ... Monday ... I racked my brain.

"You're scheduled to present at the developer conference. Tips designed to help programmers create apps for the game. Don't tell me that you forgot? You were supposed to get me a draft of your presentation yesterday."

Ah, right. Centre Terrain had an annual developer conference, predictably called Centre Terrain Open World, which was held just down the street at the Moscone Center. One of the beauties of the program was that it allowed certified developers to create applications that ran inside it. This had the dual benefit of making people feel more connected to the game, while allowing the company to add new functionality for just a pittance of what it would cost to hire full-time coders. It also meant that the virtual world was continually evolving, often in ways that were unpredictable.

"I haven't forgotten," I said, a lie. "It's coming along. I just wanted to tweak it a bit more. I'll get you a copy this weekend."

Edzard gave me a hard glare, drummed his fingers on the desk. I could tell that he was worried I'd flake. I had a history of not coming through for him. There was the time that I forgot about a dinner with the company's board of directors. Another instance when I left my augmentation glasses at a coffee shop (a very big no-no). And on more than a few occasions, I'd just neglected to come to work. Edzard had taken me to task for these, and other, infractions. He'd hit me with a few lashes of the tongue, and I got the impression that I would have been shown the door if not for the fact that I was such an ace coder. I was actually surprised when he asked me to present at the developer conference.

"Good," he said, and his fingers, which had been doing an anxious little tap dance on the desk, stopped moving. "We have a walk-through scheduled on Sunday. Here. At noon. We're planning to refine everything then."

"Yeah, I know." Another lie – I didn't know. That too had slipped my mind. "I'll be there."

Edzard nodded. "So you say you've given thought to your presentation..." He looked at me, hopefully.

"Sure. I've cooked up something really fun and informative."

"Anything you'd like to share?"

"Not yet. It's still being refined. But you're going to love it."

"Can you boil it down for me? I just want a feel for what you have planned. I'm placing a lot of faith in you. I'm a little out on a limb here."

"Look, man, I mean, it's cool, okay. But it's not there yet. I'll get you something, word of honor."

He gave me a blank stare. "See that you do." He made a waving gesture with his hand to let me know that the meeting was over. I stood and walked toward the door, opened it.

"I'll see you Sunday," Edzard barked behind me, as I stepped through entrance. "Be there."

Nika, who was still waiting outside, touched my shirtsleeve and said, "We're still on for tomorrow night, right?"

"Yes. Definitely."

Out of the corner of my eye, I spotted Edzard's face, which wore a puzzled scowl.

≈≈≈

It was 4:30. I had an hour and a half to kill until I was scheduled to meet up with Whitfield, so I walked down to the Embarcadero, sat on a park bench, and watched a gigantic cargo ship ease its way under the Bay Bridge. It was weighted down with dozens of metal shipping containers, probably at the tail end of its long and dull journey across the Pacific from China.

The weather was still pleasant, sunny, but it wouldn't last long. Not far to the west, I saw a wave of fog threatening to engulf Angel Island.

My six hours of sweeping had left me drained. My head felt groggy, lethargic. With the workday behind me, my thoughts migrated back to the Troll. I pictured him floating in and out of doors, swimming in space, smiling. I pushed these thoughts aside. I wanted my head clear, at least momentarily. I stuck my earbuds in my ears, and with a thumb selected "Trojans" by Atlas Genius off the music app. I'd been listening to that song over and over, playing it practically to death.

A jogger hurried past me. His face caught my attention. It was the Captain! I recognized him immediately. I stood and started to chase after him. But before I could take two steps, the man turned his head to one side and I got a clearer glimpse of his profile. I saw that it wasn't him after all. There wasn't even a close resemblance.

This wasn't the first time that I'd mistakenly thought I'd seen the Captain. Since the day I'd returned to San Francisco, I was *sure* I'd spotted him a number of places: drinking coffee in the Marina, eating sizzling rice soup at a Chinese restaurant. Once I thought I spied him at the gym, but when I turned, it was just my reflection in a mirror. Each time that I thought I'd seen him it was really just my mind playing tricks on me.

I sat back down on the bench and for the umpteenth time thought about the Captain. Where had he gone? What was he up to? It was difficult to reconcile the fact that he'd urged me to come home, to leave Italy, to abandon the life I'd started to map out for myself, and then he'd just disappeared. I'd toyed with the idea that he was dead, but that couldn't be. There would have been an obituary or some type of notice. Maybe he'd just dropped out, moved to somewhere out in the boonies, discarded all of his possessions, erased his electronic fingerprint, and was living the simple life. But I knew that wasn't realistic. The

Mark Richardson

Captain was a schemer and a serial entrepreneur, at least
that was the image that he'd presented to me. It was more
than likely, I'd decided, that the opportunity he'd contacted
me about had turned out not to be fully baked yet. So he was
off cooking it some more. He'd eventually pop back up and,
with a little showmanship, loop me in.
At least that's what I hoped, even if I wasn't always
honest with myself.

≈≈≈

At ten past five I walked to my favorite sushi restaurant.
I often ate there after work, not because of the quality of the
food – decent, not excellent – but because I found it
soothing. Instead of waiters, the food was dished up on sushi
boats that moved in a circle around the counter on a moat.
The meal required practically no social interaction. I didn't
even need to ask for a table, I simply grabbed an open chair.

The room was small, poorly lit, and besides myself there
was only one other patron, an old man who sat noiselessly at
the opposite side of the counter.

From the boats I selected a California roll, two pieces of
unagi, and a bowl of edamame. As I washed these down with
a cup of hot tea, a question occurred to me: Why had the
Troll contacted me? *We're going to change the world*, he'd
said. What did he mean? No answers came.

Once I'd paid my bill, I nodded to the chef, who barely
acknowledged my presence. Then using an app on my
phone, I requested a ride through the Lyft car service.

Back outside, the temperature had dropped significantly.
The sun was hidden, fog had seeped in. Moments later the
car arrived. The laconic driver wore dreadlocks and
enormous round earlobe-filling earrings. His arms were
inked with tattoos. I tucked into the backseat. We drove off.

5

ude...
How's life treating you? Better than the alternative, right? But that's your line.

Just think: one year ago at this time of day, we'd have probably been sitting in an air-conditioned conference room talking about perfecting the customer experience or improving network performance or how to maximize investor return. Boring shit, some might say, although God, not me. I'll admit it: I miss it!

Are you still in Italy? It's like you dropped off the face of the planet. No messages? Not even a single text? That's all right, you know, I can let it slide. It's not like I've held up my end of the bargain. Sometimes we all need to walk alone.

I actually have an image of where you are. I see you holed up on a beach along the Amalfi Coast. With one hand you're clutching a bottle of good red wine, while your free arm is wrapped around a hottie who only speaks Italian. Who needs to converse when you're engaged in the language of passion? Ha! Am I far off? I hope you're getting some action for a change. Sorry, dude, but it's true. Life's too short – sometimes you just need to go for it.

It's nice having some money, huh? No obligations. No worries, at least for the time being. And we're young, so why not live it up? At least I hope that's what you're doing, with your saucy little hottie.

For a while there I really got into yoga. I thought it

would mellow me out, and it did, but I grew tired of it and stopped. It's too bad because I'll tell you: I was in good shape there for a while.

Maybe this is getting too boring? I had a point. At least I thought I did. Regardless, the yoga phase is over now. Just a memory.

I've finally noticed something that you've been telling me for years. Time moves differently depending on what you're doing, doesn't it? That's another one of your tired lines. Something Einstein said, right? See, I need you around to discuss this type of stuff. Anyway, for a while there, time just seemed to inch along. Take magazine reading. I remember working my way through an article, it seemed like I'd been there for an hour or so, but when I'd finished, it had only been ten minutes. It was like someone had stopped the hands of the clock. That's just a small example, one of many. I'm not built for the life of leisure. I need days where I'm so busy that time just seems to slip past me. I arrive for work, and then next thing I know it's six. That's living for me.

What I really want to do is start another company. I like to be in charge. But you know that. The problem is I don't have any ideas. Embarrassing, I know. You can't really get funding for a start-up with no idea what product you're going to deliver. I racked my brain but nothing came to mind. I just know that I'm not fit for a corporation. The bureaucracy would kill me. Literally. The cleaning lady would come to my office one night and find me dead at my desk. "He died of boredom," the autopsy would read.

Okay, now here's the thing, the actual point of my note, it's not all fun and games. Despite my complaints above, I have found another start-up opportunity. This one has the potential to be BIG. I want to tell you about it, but I can't disclose anything. I've been sworn to secrecy. I *even signed an NDA. I did get permission to send this message, though. I wish I could tell you more.*

Christ, I'm rambling. So here's the bottom line. Dude, I need you. Hop on a plane and come home. Pronto! (See, I know a little Italian.) I really feel like you're the missing piece, the one that can kick this darn thing into another gear.

Later. Peace. Out.

- Captain.

≈ ≈ ≈

I was in Rome when the Captain's email arrived. During my time in Italy, I'd developed a routine where I drank two espressos every morning. There were various spots I'd go, but my favorite was a tiny café hidden in a side street near the Trevi Fountain. It was a little touristy, but that was okay – I got off on the energy generated by new arrivals.

I read the email twice, on my smartphone, ordered a second espresso, and read it two more times. Partway through that last reading I knew what I was going to do. I shot the Captain an email that read simply: *I'll see you tomorrow.* And then another: *Can you give me any more details?* Even before I'd left the café I'd booked a direct flight from Rome to San Francisco.

I got in touch with the friends I'd cultivated in Rome and told them I'd be going home. They took it in stride. Then, with a spring in my step, I spent a good part of the day packing up my apartment, sent a check to my landlord for more than was required to sever our lease (I didn't want any hassles), and that night ate a final meal of *pasta del mare.*

The next morning the Captain still hadn't responded to the email question I'd sent him. But that didn't stop me from boarding the jet and flying home.

≈ ≈ ≈

In the backseat of the Lyft car on the way to Whitfield's house, I reread the Captain's note, and wondered for the millionth time what had happened to my friend.

66Hit this," Whitfield said as I stepped through his front door. He thrust a plump joint under my nose. I pinched the end and dutifully obliged. My throat burned, I almost coughed, but kept it down. The smoke expanded my lungs, I held it for a few beats, eventually let it stream out my nose.

Before meeting Whitfield I'd never gotten high, never even considered it. This was despite the fact that I'd grown up in Santa Cruz, a town where the air reeked with the aroma of fine bud. Then Whitfield came along and effectively made getting stoned a requirement of our friendship. The first time I tried it I was hooked. A latent craving had been set free. I took to it like a fish to water. Plus, it suited the state of mind that I was in at the time. Just like that, I started smoking almost daily.

I handed the half-smoked joint to Whitfield. As he lifted it to his lips, some ashes escaped off the tip and floated onto his raffish, salt-and-pepper goatee. He brushed them off. In his early sixties, Whitfield had an afro so wild it looked like he'd stuck a finger in an electrical outlet. Still, he gave off a professorial air, even when working a doob.

After he'd finished toking, he passed the joint back my way and ordered, "Have another go."

"Aye, aye sir," I said, and tried to inject a sarcastic tone to my voice. I took a hit. Completely baked, I pressed the nearly finished nub out in a nearby ashtray. Two others roaches were already nestled inside.

"Let's get it on," Whitfield said. His eyes, despite being bloodshot, were focused.

≈≈≈

I'd met Whitfield through an ad I'd placed on Craigslist. It read: *Chess player seeks pawn pushing partner.*

That was two months after I'd started working at Centre Terrain. At that point I was friendless, lonely. Every night I spent holed up in my apartment getting drunk on Anchor Steam or Bloody Marys and playing chess online until I stumbled into bed around two or three in the morning. Once I fell asleep mid-game, slumped right into my chair after just a dozen moves.

The next morning I decided I needed to rustle up some type of social life – anything, simple human contact. I'd become a little reclusive and was worried that if I kept up the solo routine I'd morph into one of those filthy, crazy men who ramble up and down Market Street mumbling incoherent conversations with the voices in their heads.

"Think you can handle my game?" Whitfield said just before the first time we played. He flashed me a wicked smile, like he was some kind of chess hotshot.

He wasn't.

He was skillful, knew how to push a pawn, but couldn't quite match me. After a handful of games, he said, "We're going to need to level the playing field. Do you get stoned?"

I told him that I didn't, never even tried the stuff.

"Good. Well, you do now." He dug a joint out of a little wooden box, which was decorated with drawings of people – naked men and women – engaged in different tantric positions. By the looks of it, I guessed he'd bought the box in Chinatown. Using a match, he fired up the tip of the joint. "This shit does wonders for my creativity," he said, took a drag and passed it to me.

Sure, I could have declined, but I didn't. And his ploy worked. The weed dulled my senses just enough so that Whitfield and I were fairly equal. I still won more than I lost, but he got a few good licks in. We got together frequently, on an ad hoc basis, and played hours of speed chess. Despite our age difference, we were kindred spirits. He was a good dude.

≈ ≈ ≈

Whitfield kept his chessboard and pieces in a chest near his fireplace. As he pulled them out, I tried to determine the exact moment when I slipped from being sober to being high. It was an exercise I'd done ever since that first time I smoked pot with Whitfield. Unfortunately, I've never successfully pinpointed a tipping point. It seems there isn't a finger-snap event, more of a slow slipping.

Whitfield placed the board down on his round glass-topped kitchen table and arranged the pieces as we sat in our customary chairs. He then pushed his e-pawn two squares ahead. Unfortunately, because I was still preoccupied with examining my growing buzz, after just a few moves into the game, I hung a bishop. Whitfield hungrily snapped it up. Down a piece, I played on for a few more moves, but eventually accepted the inevitable, resigned, and we moved on to another game.

As that game progressed, a memory flukishly flashed in my head. Why I remembered that particular event is a mystery. It was a complete non sequitur. There was no reason that it popped up other than, I suspect, the weed I'd smoked had triggered a neural reaction, a firing in the brain that caused these images to materialize.

Anyway, in this particular memory I'm a boy, around six or seven, on a playground swing. My brother is swinging next to me. We're both laughing. It's a cool, gray day, like the first day of fall. In the background is my mother's voice. I can't see her or make out what she's saying, but I know it's her. What's odd is that in the memory I take my mother's perspective. I watch as my brother and I fly back and forth. So, in a strict sense, it isn't a real memory at all. Frankly, I'm not even sure it happened...

"Checkmate," said Whitfield, gleefully.

Shit. I needed to focus.

Whitfield owned a small cottage in the Bernal Heights neighborhood of San Francisco. A one-story home, the front door opened to a living area with a breakfast nook and off to the side was a small kitchen. Although the place was modest, Whitfield had sprung for custom-made cabinets and bookshelves built with Bubinga wood flown in from Africa. Not cheap. The walls were decorated with funky paintings. There were a few windows that let in a gentle flow of light.

We fought through a dozen rapid-fire games. When we finally called it quits, light from the moon had started to creep into the room, inched across the hardwood floors.

"Dude, I'm cashed," I said as we finished the last game. I tipped my king over. I'd lost much more than I'd won, which was nearly unprecedented. My brain felt mushy, as if a child had been manipulating a mound of Play-Doh.

"I wore you down," said Whitfield, and he cackled triumphantly. "Water?"

He walked to the kitchen and filled up two tall glasses. I left the dining room table, moved into his living room, and sat on a brown leather reclining chair. I pushed the seat back, kicked my legs up. Whitfield handed me a glass heavy with water and then sat adjacent to me on a sofa.

"So, my brother," he said, "what's going on with you? I'd like to believe that I've suddenly improved my game dramatically. I'm old, but not an old fool. What's on your mind?"

I rubbed my eyes with a thumb and fingertips and shook my head. Whitfield opened his eyes wider, turned his palms upward, urging me to explain.

So I told Whitfield about my encounter with the Troll. I started at the beginning: the blackness, the warm light, my feeling of euphoria and sense of belonging. I got swept away by my own story, stood up, and with my fingers pretended to draw a series of zeroes and ones in the air.

"Binary code," I said, "scrolling in the air, all around me. And some other weird shit." I described what I'd seen, the doors and the 3-D circles.

"All just floating around you?" Whitfield asked, with an inquisitive shrug.

"Yeah, that's right, more or less."

Whitfield took a sip of his water as I continued to describe what I'd seen. I told him about the doors and the appearance of the Troll. With a bit of theatrics, I stood on the leather recliner, stretched my arms up, and said, "The Troll was this tall, easy." I tried to convey the beauty of the scene, the oddness, and did my best to accurately cover every detail, left nothing out.

As I spoke, I read Whitfield's expression for a reaction, but he was stone-faced. With one hand, he slowly stroked his beard. I'd called him because I'd felt that if anyone had heard of the Troll, it would be him. He'd been a fixture in the Valley since the seventies, when he'd launched a newsletter called simply, *Tech News*. Although his journal was small potatoes when compared to other news outlets, it was widely read by tech movers-and-shakers, and as a result, Whitfield had met practically every major player in the Valley. He'd heard all the tall tales, was familiar with all the myths and legends, or at least so he'd told me.

When I finished recounting my encounter with the Troll, I retook my seat on the recliner. I sipped some water, let out a sigh. "So...?"

Whitfield sat motionless, thinking. I could practically see the gears grinding in his head. We stayed there in silence for so long that eventually I stood up, went to the bathroom, peed. When I returned, Whitfield still sat in silence. He'd crossed his legs and was rubbing his goatee. Through a window, I could just make out some city lights as they flickered.

Eventually, Whitfield spoke. "The Troll said you were connected through your neural processor, that's what you said?"

I nodded.

Whitfield stood. Both of our glasses were empty. He gathered them up, walked to the kitchen, and returned with them fully loaded. Ice cubes tinkled against the side. He handed me my glass and then sat back down on the sofa.

"So we've never really discussed your processor, have we?"

I shook my head.

"How big is it?"

"Tiny. Not even the size of a popcorn kernel."

"And it's implanted in your brain."

"Connected right to the cerebral cortex."

"And what does it do?"

"It's a dedicated processor. The only thing it does is let me navigate through the Centre Terrain gaming system faster. Every Sweeper has one installed. In fact, to be a Sweeper you *have* to have one – there's just too much network latency without it. It would be impossible to move at the speed required."

"What will they think up next, brother?"

I detected a tone of reproach.

"Each Sweeper gets a one hundred thousand dollar bonus to have the thing installed," I informed him.

"That's a lot of coin. I'm just thinking – "

I cut him off: "It's harmless. There are no side effects. Like I said, it's a dedicated processor. It interfaces only with the game."

"Tell that to the Troll," Whitfield said, with a slight lift of an eyebrow.

I started to say something but stopped myself. I had nothing to offer. We returned to silence, but this time only for a minute. Then Whitfield said, "So this Troll – could he be part of the game?"

I shook my head.

"You're sure?"

"There's no way. No one knows the game better than I do. The Troll is not part of it."

"Okay," he said, "I think you're right. Besides, this Troll, he seems familiar."

"Really?"

"He's lodged somewhere in my head, I just can't produce the knowledge right now." He stood, walked to the coffee table where he kept his tantra-decorated wooden box, opened it, and produced another joint. "Let's burn this," he said. "Maybe it will help."

We smoked the entire thing. It didn't help.

What it did accomplish, in addition to injecting me with a near comatose buzz, was to make us both hungry. So we shared an enormous bag of potato chips, ate nearly all of it.

While we munched, Whitfield flipped on the TV to PBS, and we watched an old black-and-white Bogart movie, *The Big Sleep*. Partway through I fell asleep in the recliner. At some point Whitfield shook me awake, told me to move over to the sofa, and gave me a throw blanket. As I settled into the cushions, Whitfield walked to his bedroom. I checked the time on my phone: 12:36 a.m. *Would sleep bring another visit from the Troll?* I wondered in the silence of the night.

7

I was in a piazza in Rome, although I'd never seen this actual piazza before. It was densely crowded with people, happy people, revelers, partiers. The place hummed.

Next to me was a statue. It tapped me on the shoulder and said, "Your friends are across the way, on the opposite end."

I was about to say thank you, but remembered that statues don't talk.

So I snaked my way through the crowd. It wasn't easy. People were packed as tight as sardines. *Scusi, scusi, scusi,* I repeated over and over as I pushed my way past the bodies. No one seemed to mind.

In time, I reached the other side. My friends were there, my Italian friends. *Ciao, amici!* They shouted. They were at a restaurant, seated at a long table, eating *al fresco. Pose, pose,* they said and directed me to an open chair.

"I can see why you liked it here," said a voice off to one side. I swiveled my head and saw the Captain occupying the chair next to mine.

"What are you doing here?" I asked, confused, taking time to form each word properly.

He shrugged.

"Loafing, what else?"

"Naturally."

A smile pushed the corners of his mouth, that same old gap-toothed grin. "Here comes more wine," he said, and lifted his glass.

I followed suit, raised my glass as well.

At the head of the table was the Troll. In his enormous hand he held a carafe of red wine. He worked his way around the table, filling each glass in turn, as my friends shouted, *grazie, grazie, grazie.* Despite all the pours, the carafe never emptied.

≈≈≈

When I woke, it took me a moment to register where I was. It was dark, but I could make out Bubinga wood, funky artwork – it was Whitfield's house. Then I realized that it had been a dream, just a standard old dream. Not that dreams are meaningless, but it didn't lead me to where I wanted to go. So I settled back down onto the couch.

And I knew that I wasn't any closer to finding the Troll.

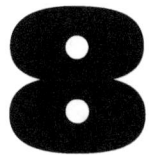

Two days after the visit from the Troll, the sound of Whitfield grinding coffee beans jolted me awake. I immediately started jonesing for my phone, eager for a data hit. My hand dropped to the floor and searched the rug until I eventually located it hidden under the edge of the sofa. With one eye still shut, I checked the time (8:50), saw I had no emails or text messages (a not uncommon occurrence), and then scanned Google News to see if anything significant had happened during the night. Nada.

I rolled over onto my back and lay motionless for a few minutes until Whitfield beckoned me over to the table where we'd played chess the night before. There he'd laid out two cups of coffee and two bowls. Each bowl contained a grapefruit. We exchanged a few words, but mostly ate and drank in silence. Eventually Whitfield broke the quiet.

"Oh, hey, I meant to tell you," he said between sips of coffee, "I managed to remember where I learned about the Troll." He squeezed the juice from his eaten grapefruit into the bowl and then drank the pinkish liquid.

"Yes..."

"Gosling told me about him, not so long ago. Said this Troll was an amazing technologist, the best he'd ever seen. Gosling went on and on about the Troll. We'd been drinking, so I thought it was just a tall tale. But maybe there was something to it?"

"Gosling?"

Whitfield shot me a cross-eyed look. "You don't know who I'm talking about?" he asked.

I shrugged.

"Larry Gosling," he continued. "Jeez. You know, sometimes I worry about you."

Whitfield had a habit of assuming an avuncular and mildly condescending tone with me. We all have our faults and I chose to overlook this one of his.

"Whatever. Just tell me, who's Gosling?"

"The Architect. He's one of the icons in the Valley." Whitfield cleared our bowls, carried them over to the sink. "I wrote a feature profile on him. God, it must have been twenty years ago now."

Whitfield pushed his chair back, stood. He walked over to the countertop and pulled a half-smoked joint out of the ashtray. He lit the end, inhaled, and offered me a hit. I waved him off.

With the smoke still buried in his lungs, his voice hoarse, Whitfield said, "I'll tell you what I'll do. I'll shoot him an email. See if I can arrange a meeting. Maybe he can give you some more information on that Troll of yours."

Sometime later we said our goodbyes and I headed for the front door, but just as my hand reached for the doorknob, Whitfield said, "Wait..." He walked slowly toward me, pulled five glass containers out of the pocket of the robe he was wearing. They were the type of containers you'd find at the grocery store, holding maybe basil or oregano or thyme. But these were packed with a different herb.

"I scored these for you." Using both of his hands, Whitfield placed the containers into my open palms, but he didn't let go. Instead, he fixed me with a serious stare. "Careful with this shit. It was cooked up by two of my friends, astrophysicists at Lawrence Livermore Labs, erstwhile classmates of mine at Berkeley. It's genetically engineered, equal parts Maui Wowie, Thai stick, and Sedona Peyote bud. They fertilize it with rhinoceros dung and have scientifically determined the optimal amount of artificial sunlight and water to use. They branded it Neil deGrasse Tyson, shortened to Da Grass. Every winter they smuggle a supply into the Australian Outback, smoke it by the bushel-load, and study the constellations."

His spiel finished, he finally released his grip, as solemnly and earnestly as if he was handing me a newly discovered parchment of the Dead Sea Scrolls.

"I'll be careful," I assured him.

He nodded and said, "Are you sure I can't talk you into taking one hit now?"

I paused, just for a second, before saying, "If you twist my arm."

From Whitfield's house I rode three separate Muni lines home, the last being the 1-California. I didn't mind riding the bus, not like some people. Let others handle the driving, it gave me a chance to think. As the 1-California eased its way past Fillmore and Gough and Polk Streets, I looked out the window and replayed the Troll's appearance in my head, tried to decipher what it meant. I could still make out the entire scene, but it was beginning to fade into just an echo.

We're going to change the world. The Troll's words danced across my mind.

After a while I got bored, slipped on my earbuds, and listened to "Trojans." Again. The tune played and I wondered if anyone could smell the absurd amount of weed that I had stored in my jacket.

After more than an hour on the buses, I was back inside my apartment. Later that day I was scheduled to eat dinner with Nika, but that was still six hours away. So with time to kill I decided to log into Centre Terrain, take a little joy ride.

The company had equipped each Sweeper with a pair of augmentation glasses and a PowerBook for home use. You couldn't predict when an emergency might occur, maybe a massive system failure, and they'd need all hands on deck.

Technically, we weren't supposed to enter the game strictly for recreational purposes, but that rule was routinely ignored.

≈≈≈

Christ, it felt good to be back inside! Roma flexed his muscles, felt a surge of strength pulsate through him. He felt drunk on the sensation of unlimited power. But where should he go? To one of the myriad forests or swamplands, perhaps explore a castle or fortified city, or maybe even go underground, into one of the caves?

Nah, too pedestrian, he thought.

Roma liked to investigate the new areas that were outside the original framework of the game, parts of Centre Terrain that had been built and installed by third-party developers. Just the previous week he'd literally fallen through a rabbit hole and into a nearly perfect replica of *Alice in Wonderland,* complete with red and white queens, a talking rabbit, and a Mad Hatter. Another Sweeper had tipped him off that someone had recently installed a 1970s version of the Playboy mansion, equipped with an imitation Hugh Hefner and the fabled grotto. Roma figured that would be a good place to start. Maybe he'd even get his rocks off?

He was about to buzz off and go in search of Hef's love shack when a Halfling materialized and blocked his path.

"*Hmmmaaa...*" the Halfling said.

It was the same peculiar, big-eyed little fella who Roma had seen before, on the roof of the pub, right after the Jett-inflicted massacre. The Halfling stood still, his unblinking eyes seeming to implore Roma to stop and engage. There was something about the Halfling that gnawed at Roma, a sense of familiarity. Had he seen him before? He didn't think so, but still, that feeling was there. Roma felt an affinity for the Halfling, an affinity that spurred him to ask, "Is there something you want? Can I help you in some way?"

"Yes, yes," said the Halfling. "There's a hole I want you to come and look at."

"A hole. In the program? Is that what you mean?"

"Yes, yes, a hole." The Halfling's eyes started to spin in a circle, as if a giant, unseen hand had grabbed him by the feet and swirled him around. After a few seconds, the pupils landed back into their normal locations and the Halfling repeated, "Yes, yes, a hole. Come with me, I will show you."

"You want me to follow you?"

"Yes. Follow me."

So Roma did. And it took only seconds until they reached their destination. The Halfling seemed to possess the same speed-of-light travel ability that was supposedly the exclusive right of the Sweepers.

"How'd you do that?" Roma asked. "Move so quickly, I mean."

The Halfling ignored the question. "Don't eat the plants," he said. "I made that mistake once."

Roma looked around and saw that they were in a field of densely packed mushrooms, mushrooms of all shapes, sizes, colors – purple and red and orange and yellow and aqua and so on. Butterflies floated through the field, softly landing on mushrooms, staying for bit before taking off and floating around again.

Cutting through the foliage was a narrow dirt path. The Halfling shuffled along the path until he got to the edge of the field. He pointed to a spot a few feet above his head, eye-level for Roma.

"There it is," said the Halfling.

Roma stepped around the Halfling so he could get a better look. It was a hole all right, by the looks of it just a run-of-the-mill tear in the program. It was small and round, shaped like a port window on a cruise ship.

"So you want me to close it?" Roma asked over his shoulder, while keeping his eyes fixed on the hole.

"No, not close it, open it."

Roma turned and faced the Halfling. "Open it?"

"Yes. So you can step through." The Halfling's eyes started to dance again, and he let out that peculiar noise, "*Hmmmaaa...*" Once his eyes settled down, the Halfling said, "Look in the hole."

So Roma did just that. He pressed the tip of his nose to the surface and gazed through. He couldn't see far, it was like there was a thick wall of fog just behind it. The fog swayed, almost imperceptibly. For a moment, it felt like Roma's eyes were playing tricks on him, but they weren't. It was real, or at least as real as anything. Roma flattened his nose against the barrier that separated him from whatever lay beyond and with unblinking eyes watched the fog rise and fall.

In time he pulled back, looked at the Halfling, and said, "What is this? What's on the other side?"

"I don't know," said the Halfling. "You need to open it and find out."

"Why don't you open it?"

"I can't. I've tried."

"And you think I can?"

"Yes."

"Okay, I'll give it a shot," Roma said.

He opened a pop-up window. He started coding. The process calmed him. He felt the joy associated with being consumed by a project. There was an unearthly quiet, an impossible absence of noise. Roma's fingers moved quickly. He lost track of time. The only thing that mattered was the task at hand, making the hole wider. It was a puzzle that he was determined to solve. But try as he might, the hole didn't expand, at least not as far as he could tell. No matter how hard he worked the circle didn't change.

It wasn't clear how long he'd been working when Roma stopped. He closed the pop-up window, examined his work. The hole looked identical. Damn. He made a mental note that the next time – and yes, there definitely would be a next time – he needed to bring a tool to measure the circle.

At that moment it hit Roma – the Halfling was no longer around.

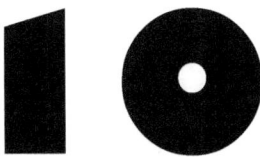

Offline and back in my apartment.

I went to the kitchen and made a ham and cheese and pickle sandwich. I pulled a bottle of beer from the fridge, returned to the living room, sat on the sofa. I decided to fire up my iPad mini, go online, and see what I could find out about the Troll. But where should I begin? It wasn't like I had a proper name, just the "Troll." I punched that word into Google, but all that came up were articles related to mythology or fairy tales or assholes on the Internet. Not helpful.

So I shifted gears.

I decided to do a little research on the man that Whitfield had mentioned, Larry Gosling. So I went back to Google. In the search window I typed "Larry Gosling." The top result was for a Wikipedia page. I clicked it. The entry was long and began:

Larry Phillips Gosling (born December 12, 1927), nicknamed "The Architect," is an inventor, author, investor, futurist, and public speaker. He was one of the first employees to join Fairchild Semiconductor in 1957, and Intel Corporation in 1968. Starting in the 1980s, he wrote a series of wildly popular books that advocated for the promotion of the transhumanist movement and his belief in life extension technologies such as nanotechnology, robotics, and biotechnology.

There was a picture of him in a black suit, white shirt, and thin black tie that took up the upper right corner of the page. He stared directly at me with intelligent, milk chocolate eyes. I pegged him at around thirty-five in the pic, maybe a little older.

The Wikipedia page had the standard sections: Biography, Early Life, Education, Career, Personal Life, Awards and Honors, and Legacy. But at the bottom there were some additional sections as well: Books, Encouraging Futurism and Transhumanism, and Future of Genetics, Nanotechnology, and Robotics. I jumped down to the bottom. According to the post, Gosling was a firm believer that at some point in this century computers will surpass people in intelligence. He believed this will be a great boon for the human race. But that's not all. According to Gosling, people and computers will merge, with humans routinely being equipped with computerized extensions to their neural cortex, robotic limbs, and nanotechnology that could effectively eliminate disease.

I was living proof that human-computer merging was already happening. Then the post got wilder.

"One day, perhaps in my lifetime, death will become an elective option," Gosling was quoted as saying in a statement before a congressional committee.

Okay...

I scrolled back up to the top of the page and skimmed through the first few sections. Gosling was born in Iowa. As a child he was obsessed with radios and spent countless hours taking them apart and then rebuilding them. He was a gifted student who attended the California Institute of Technology, where he excelled. Later he earned a PhD in mathematics at M.I.T. After leaving M.I.T. he published a number of technical papers and applied for and received half a dozen patents. Gosling had succeeded in establishing himself as one of the leading thinkers in the budding field of transistor technology, and as a result was hired by Robert Noyce to join the newly formed company Fairchild Semiconductor, in San Jose. He spent more than ten years there and then followed Noyce to Intel when that company was created. In 1979, Gosling, by then a wealthy man, retired as an engineer. But he launched a second, even more lucrative, career as an author, public speaker, and futurist. In the early 90s, Gosling expanded his career again by becoming a venture capitalist.

"I have more money than I can spend," he's quoted in a *Wall Street Journal* article, "so my first objective when picking an investment is not the potential return. No. What I'm looking for are ideas and technologies that support my belief in Transhumanism."

There was a section called Investments. Here are the last few sentences:

Gosling was the first (or "angel") investor in the online gaming company Centre Terrain, investing US$100,000. Gosling wrote the check prior to the company even being founded; it had not actually yet been legally incorporated. Despite a life of accomplishment, this one investment was the most profitable for Gosling, with its worth now at approximately $1.7 billion.

Holy crap. So Gosling was the Godfather, in a sense, for Centre Terrain. I couldn't help but be impressed with what he'd accomplished throughout his life. Fairchild and Intel are widely considered the forefathers of the Bay Area tech-boom; they literally put the silicon in "Silicon Valley." Some of the other stuff like living forever was a little too wacky for me, but who knows? Maybe he's on to something?

Just as I finished reading, Magnus Carlsen jumped up onto the sofa. He rubbed his head under my hand and meowed loudly.

"Hungry little dude?" I asked. This elicited another meow, even louder than the first.

I put down the iPad and Magnus and I shuffled off to the kitchen. There I opened a large tin of sardines and refreshed his milk bowl.

Content that Magnus was properly cared for I returned to my spot on the sofa. I flipped on the TV to a baseball game. The Giants were in the stretch drive of a pennant race. The camera zoomed into the pitcher's face. It filled the screen, every pore and every blemish magnified. His expression was a blend of fierce determination and anguish. I watched an inning before I fell asleep.

When I woke it was early evening. I hustled. Showered, shaved, brushed my teeth, dressed. My wardrobe was limited, consisting mostly of jeans and T-shirts and sweats, but I did have a white oxford, black shoes, and a blue blazer. I put those on, along with a clean pair of black jeans, and checked myself in the mirror. I nodded approvingly and my reflection nodded back.

≈ ≈ ≈

As I walked downhill from my apartment through Chinatown and into North Beach I cursed my decision not to wear an overcoat. It was frigid, damp. Wispy sheets of fog circled around me and clung to my eyelashes.

The restaurant where Nika had suggested we meet was hard to find, so hard, in fact, that I had to plug the address into my phone's Maps app. The GPS led me down a narrow alley, just a stone's throw from Washington Park, to a quaint, ivy-covered restaurant.

Nika was waiting inside. She approached me, pressed up on her toes, and gave me one of those European-style cheek-kiss greetings. It was nice and completely unexpected and brushed aside any doubts I had about whether or not this was a date.

She'd chosen more weather-appropriate attire than I had: a black wool coat that reached down to her knees. It was a classic look, even chic, and definitely different than anything I'd seen her wear before. Although she hadn't changed her look completely – black mascara was under her eyes, maybe a little less thickly applied.

"You clean up good," she said.

"You're better dressed for the weather," I titled my head, indicating her coat. "I'm not a fan of the fog."

"Really? I love it. It's one of the things that makes living here so special. It's different than everywhere else."

Before I could respond a hostess appeared and told us our table was ready. Inside the main room the light was dim, small candles scattered about. There were maybe a dozen tables, mostly full, and the room buzzed with conversation. A soothing aroma – part thyme, part garlic – danced around us. The place had a positive vibe. The hostess sat us at a table near the back. A busboy arrived with warm bread and filled a small plate with olive oil and balsamic vinegar. We munched on the bread. When a waitress arrived Nika ordered the gnocchi appetizer that she'd mentioned the day before in the Centre Terrain coffee room. She also asked for a bottle of Chianti.

"Is that okay?" she asked, and looked at me.

"Perfect."

We studied our menus. When the waitress returned to the table with our drinks, we told her that we'd decided what to eat, so she jotted down our orders.

"This is my favorite restaurant," Nika told me, once we were alone.

"So you come here a lot?"

"No. This is only my second time here."

"It's your favorite restaurant, but you've only eaten here once?" I dunked the bread into the olive oil and vinegar combination, took a bite, and washed it down with a sip of wine. It's hard to beat warm bread.

"You think that's unusual?" Nika said. "Only eating here once, that is."

"What's unusual is that you said this is your favorite restaurant, but you've only eaten here one time. That doesn't really compute."

That didn't rattle her. "It computes, all right. You see," she said, and shifted in her chair, "I made a pact with myself when I moved here – each time I ate out I'd try a new restaurant."

"Always a new one?"

"Always."

"That actually sounds like an interesting idea," I conceded. "So how long have you lived here?"

"Less than two years. I moved to San Francisco just before I joined Centre Terrain. Of course, I don't eat out every meal. But in that time that's still a lot of different restaurants. And of all the places I've been to this has been my favorite."

The gnocchi arrived. Nika was right – it was amazing. We ate quickly, quietly, except for the occasional comment, "My God, this is *so* good." Once all the gnocchi was gone we took turns using the bread to soak up the sauce at the bottom of the serving dish. When the busboy tried to clear away the plate we shooed him away; we weren't going to let a drop of that sauce escape.

"I can see why this is your favorite place," I told Nika, once we'd finally finished and the plate was removed. "I just hope the entrée is half as good. I feel a little bad, though. You broke your pact. You've now eaten at this restaurant twice."

"That's okay," she said, between sips of wine. "This is the first time I've been here with you. All the other restaurants I ate at alone."

"Alone? Every time?"

"Well," she paused, thinking. "Not every time. But nearly."

"Don't you get lonely?"

"No, not at all. I like being alone. Often prefer it. How about you? Are you the lonely type?"

I wasn't. Rather, I was something of a loner, perfectly

content with my computer or books or on a solitary walk, lost in thought. "No," I said, "I like being alone too."

"That's good." She smiled. It was a wide, toothy, welcoming smile. It was a smile that could change my world, drag me into a new plane of reality. "That means that we're both here because we truly want to be with the other person," she continued. "We're not just here because we don't want to be alone."

"That's a good way to look at it."

"It's the only way, if you ask me." Shifting gears she said, "So we've worked together all this time and I know practically nothing about you."

"We've barely even talked before."

"That's true. Why didn't you ever ask me out?"

The question stumped me. The real answer was because she'd given me absolutely no indication that my asking her out would have been a welcome event. In fact, she'd totally and completely ignored me. I had the clear impression that she wanted me to keep my distance. So not knowing what to say I swirled the wine in my glass, admired it, and then drank what was left.

Nika pushed forward. "I was told you spent a year in Italy."

"That's right."

"And before that you had some type of breakdown, right?"

I diverted my eyes. How had she known that? It was true that I'd had a minor breakdown, although I preferred to think of it as an existential event. But I'd told no one. It was impossible that Nika could know this had happened.

"How did you know that?" I asked.

Nika shrugged. "You told me once, didn't you?"

She was lying, we both knew it. But I didn't press the point.

"Anyway, how was Italy?" Nika asked, pushing the

conversation onto more comfortable territory. "What did you do?"

"Loafed, mostly."

"Loafed? What do you mean?"

This was going to require another drink. I took the bottle, freshened up Nika's glass, and then filled mine nearly to the rim.

"You were going to give me your thoughts on loafing," Nika reminded me.

"Loafing. Okay. So I actually got the idea from a book, *The Razor's Edge*. Do you know it?"

She shook her head.

"It's great, you should read it. Anyway, a character in the book, Larry, after the war he decides that all he wants to do is loaf. So he goes to Europe and that's what he does."

This was a cursory description of the book. Larry does loaf, but it's more than that. He goes on a spiritual journey, questions our cultural focus on materialism, and tries to determine for himself what is really important. But it's boiled down as loafing.

"He loafs?" Nika asks.

"That's right."

"So you read the book and it inspired you to do nothing."

"More or less." I took a sip of wine. "I actually read the book ten times."

"Ten?"

"It was practically the only thing I read while I was in Italy. I'd finish it and then put it down. Sometimes just for a day, other times much longer. But eventually I'd pick it up again."

Nika frowned and tilted her head to one side, mouthed the words – *ten times*.

"You're compulsive."

"Maybe a little," I conceded. "Anyway, I came up with my own broad-stroke lifestyle theory. Want to hear it?"

"Fire away." Her voice had a touch of apprehension.

"Okay. So there are two strains of thought," I started. "One says we need to 'do.'" I made air quotes. "That's what sets us, people, apart. A dog, a cat, a rat, a bird, even the dolphin or elephant – they're destined just to be."

"To be or not to be..."

"Right. That's the other strain of thought. Some people might say, 'I kind of like being. I'm happy just to be alive.'"

While we talked, my gaze roamed to the side of her head, to the spot where her missing ear should be. I tried, casually, to peek through the strands of her red hair, to get a better look. But she must have felt the heat of my stare, because with one hand she self-consciously pushed the hair tighter on her head, so I diverted my eyes.

"I get that," Nika said, "so what about doers?"

"Doers are all about challenges, awareness – ambition. They want to be more than a simple animal. For them, enlightenment comes from accomplishing something, making a mark. They reject the idea of just being."

"That seems pretty straightforward. So let me jump ahead. You were a doer and decided to give just being a try."

The waitress arrived carrying a tray that contained our entrées. She placed the plates in front of us, sprinkled ground pepper on our pasta, and then shredded some parmesan cheese. Bing, bang, boom, and she's gone.

I took a sip of wine. It's the second drink that always hits me. I could feel the liquid slide down my throat and then upward, into the nooks and crannies of my brain. The buzz made me feel a little more alive.

"More or less," I said, picking up on where the conversation had dropped off. "Although there are different levels of doing. Don't confuse me with Picasso or Lincoln."

"Don't worry, I won't," she said, and dabbed her mouth with a cloth napkin. "But you were a goal oriented person? I can see that. You're an amazing programmer."

"You've never seen me program."

She put her fork down, looked me square in the eye. "Come on. Of course, I have. Every day at work." She pointed her forefinger at her temple and spun it, the universal sign of *cuckoo*. She smiled playfully. "False modesty doesn't suit you. You're amazing, the best I've ever seen."

I could feel myself blushing.

"How'd you get your start, programming, that is?" she asked, while she resumed eating.

I told her how I'd become enamored with computers and coding back in middle school.

"So I gather that's when you first became a doer, as you call it."

"No," I said, and drank some more wine. "It really started – the doing – back when I was six."

"Six?"

"Yeah, that's when I started playing chess."

"Chess?"

I nodded. "That's right. For a time I thought I wanted to be a professional chess player. I was actually a little maniacal about it."

"There are professional chess players?"

"Of course. Some do fairly well, financially, the very top players."

"So what happened?"

"One day I just gave it up."

We talked some more about chess and why I abandoned my dream of being a professional player. I explained that although I no longer took the game seriously, I still enjoyed playing for fun. I didn't tell her about Whitfield.

"So you do play now," she echoed.

"Yeah, I do. I gave it up for a few years, but picked it up again when I hit my twenties."

It was Nika's turn to sip her wine. "You like mental challenges."

"I do. Or I did. I liked solving problems," I said with a shrug. "Anyway, I was a better programmer than I ever was a chess player."

"Everything is in the past tense. You're *still* an amazing programmer. Our jobs at Centre Terrain – that's not doing, in your book?"

"No. Not really. To me, it's just a job. It's not loafing, but it's not *doing*."

"You worked for a start-up once, right? Was that doing?"

I nodded. "Definitely."

"Is that something you'd like to do again, start a company, I mean?" She raised an eyebrow, which quickly fell back into place.

I gave her a half-hearted shrug. "I don't know. We'll see," I said, although clearly the correct answer was yes, at least it had been when the Captain contacted me. I caught myself scanning the restaurant, looking for the Captain, before shaking my head clear and pulling myself back into the moment.

Nika had absorbed my reply in silence.

We finished our food. The plates were cleared away, and we ordered dessert, tiramisu and cappuccinos. The lights had been dimmed even lower, and the room was pleasantly dark. I could hear faint music over the sound system; Dean Martin singing "Volare." All the tables were full. The crowd was varied – old and young, clean cut and scraggily. San Francisco is a melting pot, a boisterous mix of nationalities. But the variety is also a little deceiving. I was sure that nearly everyone seated was in some way associated with the tech industry. And gentrification had taken over. The city's neighborhoods still maintained their distinct characteristics, but it didn't feel authentic. For a moment I imagined what North Beach had been like decades earlier, when Joe DiMaggio was playing black-top baseball with his brothers.

Once the dessert arrived we took turns digging out bites with our spoons.

"So getting back to what we were talking about earlier," said Nika. "Being versus doing. Have you come to any conclusions?"

"Which is better, you mean?"

"Yeah. For you."

"The jury's still out."

"But Centre Terrain might not be forever? Someday you might want to do something else, something more?" A variation of the question that she'd asked me earlier.

I told her I had no plans, but you never know.

"I've talked a lot about myself," I said. "You've told me nothing about yourself."

With a hand she brushed off my remark. "Later."

She finished her cappuccino and leaned across the table, toward me. I got a whiff of her perfume, which smelled like apricots. It had a distinct aroma, and it made my heart pump a little faster. In a hushed voice she said, "I'd like to try loafing." She smiled. "Maybe you can give me a little demonstration?"

"Sounds great."

Great indeed, perfect, in fact. Was this really happening? Nika and I on a date, Nika wanting to spend more time with me: unreal. But it had happened. And I decided that the best approach was to take it slow, get to know her, build the foundation of a real relationship. Then who knew where it could lead?

As these thoughts did a tap dance in my brain Nika leaned even further forward. My heart revved faster until I felt it might burst through my chest cavity. "But first," she said in a husky whisper. "We need to get to know each other better. Let's go to bed."

12

Chess-loving computer nerds aren't typically lucky with the ladies. Growing up I was no exception. In my high school I glanced at my female classmates with silent yearning. None of my friends were girls. I don't remember having a real conversation with one. Since I had no idea how to act on my desires I masturbated avidly.

But the summer after graduation things changed...

That was the year I started caddying. For me it was a perfect summer job. I could choose to get to the golf course early – say six – and go out with a morning foursome, and then if I wanted, hook up with another group of golfers in the afternoon. But I almost never took that approach. Instead, I skipped the morning and arrived at the caddy shack at around noon. Back then I stayed up late, coding until two or three in the morning. Then I slept 'till ten.

An advantage of carrying bags in the afternoon – in addition to being able to sleep in – was that's when the women typically teed off. I preferred caddying for women: they were usually less intense than the men, and used fewer clubs. They'd opt for a three wood off the tee, a seven wood on the fairway, wedge to the green, and then a putter.

Since the job wasn't mentally taxing I was free to ruminate about what I'd worked on the night before. I also appreciated the afternoon light on the golf course. The low-hanging sun would hit the trees and stretch their shadows far along the grass.

One day, at the start of June, after my loop (that's what we called completing eighteen holes) was done, one of the women golfers asked me if I could help her take her bags home. "They need to be cleaned," she said, "and the last time I had them do it here they did an awful job. So I'm going to take 'em somewhere else."

It was an unusual offer, one I hadn't heard before.

"Come on," she said. "The bag is heavy. I'll tip afterward."

"Okay." It seemed easy enough.

She was young, at least for the crowd at the club, mid-thirties. She wore a golf outfit with a white skirt. Her thigh muscles were pronounced, her nose slightly freckled.

Her house was just a few miles from the course. Once we arrived, I carried the bags inside. She opened the fridge and got me a bottle of water. Then she said, "Just hold tight, I'm going to get your tip."

She disappeared into the back of the home. A few minutes later I heard water running, what sounded like a shower. That struck me as odd. I cooled my heels for a half an hour until she re-appeared. Her hair was wet and slicked back. She only wore a towel, cinched just below her armpits. In her right hand she had two twenties. She extended the bills toward me and said, "Sorry for the wait. Here you go." But when I grabbed the money she didn't let go. Instead, she pulled herself closer until our bodies touched. She pushed up on her toes, kissed me. Her hand released its grip on the towel and it dropped to the ground with a satisfying swoosh.

The sex was eye-opening, lustful. I was still a little sweaty and smelled like cut-grass and sand, which made it seem animalistic.

We saw each other throughout that summer. When she was free I'd stop by after caddying, shower, and we'd have athletic sex. She'd recently gone through a divorce, and I seemed to fit what she needed, a lump of clay she could sculpt for her needs. I learned the meaning of that old line: sex is only dirty if you're doing it right.

Sometimes after we'd slept together she'd have to run out and would leave me alone in her home. I'd stretch out on her bed, maybe take a nap. Or I'd stare at a hand-carved wooden statue in her bedroom. It stood five-feet tall. She'd told me she'd bought it in Africa. "She's some type of deity," she'd once explained. I would look at the deity, she would look back at me with hypnotic eyes, and time slowly ticked away.

≈ ≈ ≈

Back in San Francisco, in my bed with Nika, her head resting on my shoulder and her naked body pressed against mine, I thought about that wooden statue. I wondered what had happened to the woman from the golf course. People flow into your life and then just as easily slip away. And the truth is that since that summer sex had been an exceptionally rare – nearly nonexistent – occurrence for me. My mind conjured up the smell of grass and the soothing sight of afternoon sunshine. Then I considered golf courses. They are strange things, aren't they? Artificial plots of manicured nature; sometimes plopped down in the middle of a city or a bedroom community.

Nika gave me a playful shake. "Hey – where'd you go?" she asked.

"On a golf course," I said.

A puzzled expression spread across her face. I pulled her closer, kissed her, and we screwed again, this time with even more urgency than before.

13

I slept remarkably well that night. It was a mellow and dreamless sleep, blissfully quiet, that is until I heard a ringing noise followed by a vibration. Both came in consistent intervals – *ring, buzz ... ring, buzz ... ring, buzz ... ring, buzz ... ring, buzz.* It sounded like an old time telephone. And with the fifth ring I realized that's exactly what it was – a telephone. I was jolted out of my deep slumber just in time to grab my iPhone off the nightstand and answer it.

"Hello..." I managed to force out in a hushed tone.

The warm feeling induced by my peaceful slumber started to ebb. My eyes adjusted to my surroundings. I was in my bedroom. There were my jeans on the ground, right next to Nika's black thong. My bureau was against the wall and the French doors that separate the bedroom from the living room were open. Nika, naked under the covers, was still asleep in the bed next to me.

"Hello. This is the personal assistant for Mr. Larry Gosling," said an exceptionally efficient sounding woman. Based on her voice, I pegged her as late forties, a polyester slacks and sensible shoes type of gal. No funny business allowed with this one. The trains would always run on time. "Mr. Gosling would like to see if you're free this afternoon to meet in at his home in Atherton. How does three o'clock work for you?"

So Whitfield had managed to reach Gosling.

"What time is it now?" I asked, still making an effort to keep my voice low.

"Six in the morning."

"Six? That's a little early to call someone, isn't it?"

"Not for Mr. Gosling." I could hear her take a breath. "Now – does three o'clock work for you?"

I told her I needed to check my calendar, although I didn't really. I knew I was scheduled to meet Edzard and work on the deck for my Centre Terrain Open World presentation, but...

"Three o'clock is just fine," I heard myself say.

"Great, we'll see you then."

Before she could hang up I breathed into the receiver, "Wait. I don't know where to go. And I don't have a car."

"That's no problem," said Miss Efficient. "We'll send a car. Please be waiting outside your front door at two fifteen. That should allow for ample time to make the drive down from San Francisco."

"Do you need my address?"

"We know where you live."

Of course you do.

≈≈≈

The call with Miss Efficient had lasted only a couple of minutes, but I was wide awake and had little hope of falling back asleep. Not wanting to disturb Nika, I slipped out of bed, stealthily pulled a robe out of the closest, and walked to the living room, closing the French doors behind me. Magnus Carlsen was asleep on one end of the sofa. He didn't rise when I sat in the opposite corner.

Normally, the first thing I did each morning was brew a pot of coffee. But the coffee bean grinder made an ungodly racket, so I decided to put that off until after Nika was up. Instead, I logged onto my iPad – again – and went to Google – again – and plugged Nika's name into the search engine.

Despite the fact that we'd worked together a year and she'd occupied a special role in my sexual fantasies, I hadn't taken the time to really research her. Why bother? I'd never imagined that she'd want to spend time with me, it was better just to keep it all make-believe.

The search came up empty. There were apparently no photographs or news articles or any of the other random online information that most people accumulate during their lives. I went to Facebook to see if she had a profile. She didn't. LinkedIn was the same result. Twitter: no. She had no online presence, at least not as far as my rudimentary search could uncover.

So what to make of that? Nothing, I decided. I was sure that if we spent more time together I'd learn where she grew up, the names of her friends, who she voted for in the last election, and even funny anecdotes about her past. All the banal humdrum things people unload on you when you get to know them better. But really, at that point, did it matter? A beautiful, sensual, mysterious, woman had decided to have loud sex with me; a one-eared temptress who'd practically stepped out of the pages of a Murakami novel. I closed the iPad and reasoned it wasn't wise to risk ruining my good fortune by examining it too close.

14

Nika slept until ten-ish and then spent another forty-five minutes showering. By the time she was finished I was so famished that I suggested we eat brunch at a restaurant I frequented down at the edge of the Tenderloin. The place was a greasy spoon, but it had hearty meals. Inside it smelled like fresh coffee and pancake syrup.

"So what's it going to be?" our waitress asked, and looked first at me and then Nika. She had the nervous, impatient energy of a woman responsible for a room full of tables.

"Well, dears?" the waitress demanded, toe tapping, when we didn't immediately answer.

I ordered the huevos rancheros and home fries, while Nika just got toast and a bowl of fruit.

As we ate, my mind floated back to the previous night, and the assorted and provocative positions that Nika had contorted herself into. In total, we'd enjoyed three separate lovemaking sessions, each one more adventurous than the last.

Partway through my second cup of coffee, in a sheepish mood, I asked Nika: "So what do you see in me?"

She didn't respond, just shook her head like it was the oddest question she'd ever heard.

Why'd she propose we go out to dinner? I inquired. Why that day?

Everyone needs to eat, she told me.

"So you make a habit of inviting men out?"

"I told you, for a year I ate alone, almost every night. You think too much, you know that?" There was a twinge of irritation in her voice. But she softened, a devilish smile formed in one corner of her mouth, a smile that soon spread across her face like a shadow. "The truth, you want to know the truth?"

I nodded.

"I could tell you were going to be fantastic in the sack. I just *had* to have you."

≈≈≈

An hour later we sat on a park bench in Aquatic Park. It was another perfect day, and people were out in force – jogging, throwing a football, lying on the grass, even swimming in the frigid bay. We let the sun warm our faces and I directed my gaze toward the Golden Gate Bridge.

"So this is loafing?" Nika said.

"It sure is."

"I could get used to this."

"Addictive, isn't it."

Eventually we roused ourselves off the bench and walked back into the city, down Polk and then up Sacramento until we landed at the top of the hill, where my apartment was situated. As we slowed, a car pulled to a stop along the curb. I checked the clock on my phone, it read 2:15.

Miss Efficient – I thought. *Not a second early or late.*

But it wasn't the type of car I'd expected. For some reason, I'd imagined that Gosling's assistant would have ordered up a black limo, a land whale, one of those cars with tinted windows that seem to take up half the block as it dramatically eases down the street.

This car was nothing like that.

For starters, it was smallish. If I had to guess, I'd say it was a Toyota of some type. It was blue with four doors. It reeked of practicality, except for one thing, there was no driver. After it had executed a perfect parallel parking job, Nika looked into the passenger window and said, "What is *this*?"

"It looks like a robotic car."

"Robotic car?"

"Yeah, when I was at Stanford I knew a guy who'd worked on a prototype. He believed that in a few decades all cars would be driven by computers. In time, people will come to view our present-day freeways the same way people now look back on the Wild West. The roads will be free of drunk drivers, texters, etc. But I thought an actual working model was still a few years away."

I walked from the front to the back and kicked the tires with admiration. "This is *very* cool."

"More like very scary. I'd never get in that thing."

"Come on," I said and wrapped an arm around her, gave her shoulder a gentle squeeze. "You'd be safer in here than if either you or I drove."

"Really?"

"Sure. Absolutely. It must be tweaked out with multiple radar sensors, cameras, a state-of-the art GPS system..."

Cutting me off, the passenger window lowered all the way down and the car spoke in a voice that sounded like it came right out of a 1950s sci-fi flick.

-*Good. Day*...Pause.

-*I. Am. Gos-ling's. Car*...Pause.

-*En-ter. Please.* The rear door unlocked.

Nika looked my way. "So it talks. And apparently it's talking to us."

"It's actually talking to me. Did I mention that I have an appointment this afternoon?"

She shook her head.

"Sorry. It must have slipped my mind."

- *En-ter. Please,* the car repeated. If Gosling's team

could build a car that can drive itself then why couldn't they give it a more appealing voice, something cooler? The obvious choice would be Morgan Freeman, but he's such a clichéd voiceover. Personally, I would have opted for someone who sounded like Jennifer Lawrence.

-En-ter. Please...Pause.

-En-ter. Pul-ease! The car was getting more forceful.

"Look, I'm sorry," I said, and looked at Nika. "But I have to go. Okay?"

Nika said that was fine, she should go herself. As she looked on, I slid into the car's backseat and sat down. The door closed by itself. The lock clicked into place. The car spoke:

-Seat. Belt. Please.

I strapped myself in. The car pulled away from the curb. I gave Nika a wave. I was off.

We (the car and I) rolled downhill. At the end of the block was a stop sign. The car executed a perfect stop; it even waited as two pedestrians crossed the street. We turned left onto Larkin, another left onto California, and then a right onto Jones. So far so good, the car had even picked the quickest route to the freeway.

On the dashboard was an instrument panel with a graphic display that showed all the other cars around us. It followed their movements. I even caught an image for a bicycle delivery rider who weaved recklessly in and out of traffic.

After leaving Nob Hill we worked our way through the Tenderloin, across Market Street, and eventually ended up on 280 heading south.

"This is spectacular," I said out loud, even though there was no one there to hear it.

The car handled itself like a dream. The only thing that concerned me was the other drivers on the road. Every now and then I'd catch someone gawking as the driver-less car raced past. Most of the gawkers got distracted, wide-eyed, like they'd spotted the headless horseman. Some of the cars drifted into our lane, but no problem, our robotic vehicle eased off the gas and kept a safe cushion between us and the wayward vehicle.

I'd been on the freeway for a minute or two when some music kicked on. Actually, music isn't the right word. It was Muzak, an easy listening instrumental arrangement. Someone had bastardized Nirvana's, "Smells Like Teen Spirit." Ripped the heart right out of the song and splattered it on the upholstery.

I hate Muzak.

It reminded me of a scene from *Saturday Night Live*. Paul Simon, as a young man, makes a deal with the devil. The devil promises to make him rich and famous, which happens. Flash forward thirty years or so and an older Simon walks onto an elevator. Inside is an awful Muzak version of one of his song's, probably "Bridge Over Troubled Water." I don't remember. The devil reappears and informs Simon that the elevator and the tune are his personal hell. He can never leave. *Brou ... ha ... ha ... ha!*

With some time to kill, I pulled my smartphone out of the back pocket of my jeans, opened the browser, and checked the news. Nothing caught my eye. So I looked at the weather app – clear skies for the foreseeable future. The calendar read September 30. Using my checkbook app, I looked at the balance in my account. No problems there. Then I opened my chess app and started a game. I pushed my king's pawn forward two squares. The machine responded with e5. I countered with f4, the King's Gambit, a tactical jungle, normally a suicide mission against the brute calculating might of a computer, which years ago leaped past even the strongest grandmasters in playing ability. But I was in a combative mood.

Bring it. Let's see where this leads...

15

When I was ten I painted a large black and white chessboard on the ceiling of my bedroom. It was directly over my pillow. After my parents tucked me in I would stare up at the board, spellbound, until eventually my eyelids got heavy and dropped shut. Then I'd see a shadowy outline of the board floating around the blackness. When I fell asleep, I dreamed about rooks and bishops and pawns and hopscotching knights.

By the time I was eleven I'd been playing chess for five years, and with real dedication for three years. I'd memorized hundreds of opening variations, played through thousands of grandmaster games, and participated in tournaments across the country. To say I was serious about the game would be like saying a bird was serious about flying. I pushed aside all other extracurricular activities and focused exclusively on becoming a stronger player.

My parents were somewhat concerned with my obsessive preoccupation, but more supportive. My father, who had taught me the game, was a strong player. We played thousands of blitz games together. By the time I was nine-and-a-half, I started beating him consistently. I was on my way to being a chess grandmaster, one of the world's top players, perhaps even World Champion. Or so I thought.

I was twelve when I played my last chess tournament. It was a regional event, held in Santa Monica, pitting the strongest pre-teens in the West against each other. The players with the top results would be invited to participate in the U.S. Junior Open Chess Championship. I played eight games, of which I lost seven and drew only one. The losing was brutal, of course, painful behind description. But it wasn't just getting beaten that was so discouraging, it was how I lost. There were no obvious blunders, no hung pieces or easy mates. It was hard for me to even pinpoint the exact faulty moves that had led to defeat. My opponents had just methodically out maneuvered me; they had a deeper understanding of the subtleties of the game. They played with machine-like precision.

After I resigned against my final opponent my father took me to lunch on the Santa Monica boardwalk. As we ate corndogs he said, "I thought you played very well. Those are some of the best young players in the country. They train, have coaches, maybe you just need to get a little better prepared?"

I nodded. I was studying the wooden boards below my feet. They roughly resembled the outlines of a chessboard – at least in my mind – pieces moved into position, opportunities presented themselves.

"Now that you have this under your belt," my father said, "I'm sure you'll do better next year."

I nodded again. My gaze remained on the pieces I saw below. I marshaled my forces, positioned them for the kill, but then looked on as they got overwhelmed and were conquered by a superior army.

My father, probably noticing my fixation, tugged my shirtsleeve and said, "Come on. Let's go take a walk along the beach."

When we returned home I stored all my chess books on the top drawer of my closet shelf. I painted over the board on my ceiling. But when I slept I still saw the 64-squares, their ghostly image floated on the surface of my closed eyes. During the day, chess positions would swim in my head, usually the very positions that I played and lost in Santa Monica. I tried to replay the games, to produce better results, but each time I just failed again.

This stretched on for months.

In an effort to clear my head, I completely abandoned the game. My father, not appreciating what I was experiencing, encouraged me to continue playing. He believed that it was just a matter of time until I would equal and then surpass the players who'd beaten me. But I knew he was wrong, I knew that I would never be able to match their strength. I just knew it. So I pushed the game aside. And that was okay. In time, my mind cleared. I was happy. But something was missing. I felt rudderless, adrift – empty.

Chess grandmasters have a term they use when they're focused on analyzing the possibilities of a particularly complex position; it's called being in "The Tank." Getting lost inside the spiraling vortex – the incomprehensible complexities of the game – is one of its appeals. Time stands still. You feel connected to a force that's bigger than yourself.

I didn't miss the competition, but I did miss The Tank.

Then one day I discovered a replacement. Or maybe it's more accurate to say that it discovered me. I was at a bookstore and I saw a book on computer science. I don't remember consciously seeking it out, I just happened to walk down a particular aisle, my hand went to that book, and I started reading it. I spent an entire afternoon at the bookstore studying that book. When I finished, I bought other books on computers and programming, took them home, read them as well. Soon I started coding, just puttering away, but quickly I became serious. Before long I was spending more time writing code than I'd ever spent playing or studying chess. I was hooked. And I was good. I had an aptitude for programming that far exceeded whatever innate ability I had for playing chess. I'd found an avenue for channeling my mental energy. I continued coding daily, without interruption, until the day that Polpo shut its doors.

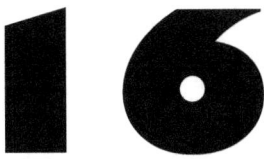

Gosling's house was located in a secluded, semi-forested area. Everywhere I looked it was green. Songbirds chirped loudly. There was a black cast iron gate, easily ten feet tall, at the front entrance. The robotic car pulled to a stop, communicated electronically its desire to enter, and the gate slid open.

We drove down a long and curvy driveway. The expansive yard was gracious, perfectly manicured. There wasn't an uncut blade of grass or a misplaced leaf. Two ducks floated on a little pond. The scene reeked with serenity.

In short order we made it to Gosling's home. The car noiselessly pulled to a stop and I stepped out. The house wasn't the monstrosity that I'd expected. Sure, it was large, with a three-car garage, but tasteful. I'd anticipated a mini-castle – muscular with an old-world sensibility, tacky. Instead, the building was understated yet stylish. It was low and long with stone walls and a black tile roof. There were lots of windows and two chimneys. In front, there were roses and bougainvillea and impatiens exploding with color. Humming birds and fat bumble bees flitted among the flowers.

It smelled wonderful.

The weather was twenty degrees warmer than back in San Francisco. I stretched and felt the sun as it warmed the kinks out of my body.

The house's front door opened and out walked a woman. She glided confidently toward me, with long, purposeful strides. She was tall, although not abnormally so, just tall enough that it was the first thing I noticed. The second thing I noticed was her hair: so black it shined, and pulled back in a bun. She stopped a few feet in front of me, for a beat or two she seemed to regard my presence, then smiled concisely and said, "Welcome."

That voice, that voice. Could *this* be Miss Efficient?

Late forties: no. I pegged the woman who stood in front of me as late twenties.

Brown polyester pants: no again. She wore a black dress, not provocative but tailored just right.

Sensible shoes: sort of. They were black flats, stylish, yet looked comfortable.

It's funny how so often the image I create in my mind when talking to someone on the phone rarely matches reality. I'd pictured a frumpy older woman, but was confronted by a put together young lady. Still, on both the phone and in person she emitted an air of competence.

"We spoke this morning," she said, and extended her hand. We shook, efficiently – two pumps. "I'm Priya, Mr. Gosling's assistant."

"Nice to meet you."

"Follow me." She led me around the house.

≈≈≈

The backyard of Gosling's home was filled with a Japanese garden so perfect that it looked like it belonged in an imperial palace. There was a teahouse, ponds (including a koi pond), waterfalls, bonsai trees, and stone replicas of temples. It was exquisite. The sky was cloudless and sunlight twinkled off the water.

Attached to the house was a large wooden canopy covered with ivy. Under the canopy was a round patio table with four chairs. Sitting in one chair was an elderly man. He had a full head of bushy gray hair that I assumed was built with the help of hair plugs. If my assumption was right, it was a top-notch job. He wore a gaudy Hawaiian shirt, khaki shorts, flip-flops, and black Ray Bans. In that getup he looked like a member of the Beach Boys still trying to cling to his glory years. Although that's not exactly right, because the man in front of me was too old for even that geriatric crowd. But he didn't give off an elderly sensation. It seemed that being in your eighties nowadays is not what it used to be.

But he did have a cane. And he used it to push himself out of his chair. He sprang upright and with impressive dexterity stepped toward me. Priya led me out of the sun and under the cool shade of the canopy.

"Hello," he said, and extended a hand. We shook. "Call me Gosling."

I told him I was happy to meet him.

"Wonderful, please sit." With the end of his cane he pointed toward the chair across from where he had just risen.

"Now what will you have to drink?" Gosling asked, as he got situated back in his seat.

I told him water.

"Nonsense. Its happy hour and I refuse to drink alone. We'll have two Mojitos," he said, with a glance toward Priya.

She nodded and walked deliberately through a back door to go and fulfill our orders.

≈≈≈

The Mojito was damn good. We quickly polished off our drinks and engaged in idle conversation, including a prolonged discussion about the beauty of California's dry and sunny weather, a favorite pastime of all residents of the state, especially transplants. In time, Gosling called for Priya and asked her to fetch us up another round.

"So I'm an investor in the company you work for," Gosling said, between sips.

Yeah, and it made you filthy rich. "I read that."

"Not that I care about online gaming. It seems a complete waste of time."

"It can be a time waster, that's for sure."

"I was intrigued by the processor." He swirled the ice cubes in his glass. "Did it hurt to get it installed?"

"No, really, it didn't."

"And it works? It allows you to work through the game, to code faster?"

I nodded.

Even through his sunglasses, Gosling's eyes seemed to twinkle. He looked rather jolly. The old guy was quickly growing on me. Or maybe it was the Mojitos?

"Do you understand how it works?"

I shook my head. "No. Not really."

"And you consider yourself a technologist?" he teased, although that twinkle still remained in his shaded eyes.

"I'm more of a software guy."

"Would it be all right if I explained?"

I told him to go ahead.

"So," Gosling began, "I'll try not to be too pedantic. You understand what a microprocessor is, am I right?"

"Yes. Of course."

He pressed his eyes shut and then re-opened them. He cleared his throat, sighed, and got rolling.

"Microprocessor chips," he said, "are made out of fairly thick silicon. Resting on top of that chip are integrated circuits. These are very small, minute, thousands of times thinner than a human hair. It's the integrated circuits that are really the brains of the device. The chip is there to support them. Typically a processor is installed in a computing device – a laptop, cell phone, tablet, or what have you – and the chip is large enough that it allows robots to pick it up and install it in the device. The integrated circuit is too small for even a robot to properly install. Without the chip, it couldn't be done."

He shifted in his chair, and then continued.

"But what works for a computer won't work in a human. Do you think an entire microprocessor could be installed inside a person?" Before I could respond, Gosling answered his own question, "Of course not. It's too rigid. But what the team at Centre Terrain figured out – and by team, I suspect it would be more accurate to say the Troll – was that they could discard the supporting chip, and just use the integrated circuit, which was so thin it's flexible. This flexibility allows it to form onto a curved surface, in your case, the contours of your brain."

"Now although a computer and the human body are very different, there are also similarities. One is that the human body, just like a computer, is electrical." He must have caught the quizzical look on my face, because he lifted a hand as if to assure me that what he said was correct. "Oh yes," he continued, "the ions in our bodies communicate in ways that closely resembles the electrical circuits in a microprocessor. Once information is gathered through our external interfaces – the skin, eyes, ears, etc. – it is chemically transmitted to the brain, which then interrupts that data and determines how we should respond, if at all."

He paused, licked his lips.

"Do you know how many pattern recognizers there are in the typical human brain?" asked Gosling

"No idea." The term was a new one for me, although I could deduce what it meant.

"Three hundred million – give or take. Each person builds up his or her own. But eventually, we fill those recognizers up. That's why it's easier for a child to learn a new language – they literally have more room in their brains to add information. In time, however, with miniature gateway processors connected to our brains, we'll be able to dramatically extend the amount of data that each person can store. And hopefully, improve our cognitive ability."

Gosling stopped to take a drink. I joined him and we both emptied our glasses. I was encased by a pleasant buzz.

"Now where was I? Oh yes – the human brain. It's so intricate that some people argue it's the most complex system in the known universe. And we've not even begun to understand how it works. How does the brain generate thoughts? Or dreams? Or store memories? Unsolved riddles. How does the brain work on the cellular level? How do neural circuits function? We're just now at the beginning stages of deciphering how the brain functions. And until we can answer these questions, it isn't feasible to think that we can connect our brains to a computing device and expect the two things to work together. That chip in your head, it shouldn't work."

"But it does."

Gosling smiled. "Don't get me wrong. I am firm believer in the long-term promise of cognitive enhancers like the ones you and your co-workers are successfully demonstrating today. I believe eventually they'll be commonplace. I'd venture to guess that by the end of this century they'll be more ubiquitous than eyeglasses."

"You think so?"

"Without a doubt. It's just that it shouldn't work today."

"But it does," I repeated.

"Yes, so you tell me. And I believe you. I've also examined the data that your company has provided me. I've seen the results myself. But that still doesn't resolve the fact that it *shouldn't* work. It's a technological leap, no doubt, but one that should not occur for at least another twenty years. In time, we'll map out the brain and our cells. We'll do this sufficiently enough so that we can closely link the human body to computing devices. We'll effectively become almost interchangeable with technology, another type of hardware to be upgraded and improved."

He lifted an eyebrow. "Do you know," he asked, "that we haven't been able to replicate those integrated circuits now lodged in your brain?"

I shook my head.

"We've taken it apart and reverse engineered it and yet still can't develop a device that can be used in any function outside of that game. How it works is beyond our understanding."

"So how do you explain the fact that it does work?"

He paused before responding, built up the suspense. "The Troll," he said.

We were then interrupted by Priya, who walked through the sliding glass doors pushing a large cart that held two more cocktails, and a kingly assortment of appetizers. There were black tortilla chips and a bowl of guacamole, pita bread and hummus, mixed nuts, grapes, small candy bars, to name a few. As Gosling looked on, I helped Priya place the food on the table. Once that was done, Priya handed Gosling his drink, I took mine, and she was gone.

≈≈≈

Gosling and I sampled from the smorgasbord. The grapes and a chunk of blue cheese were particularly good.

"So, the Troll," said Gosling, between bites. "A freak." He slid a wrinkled hand through his hair, paused, apparently gathering his thoughts. "He was ugly as all get-out, but intellectually superior. They don't make 'em like that anymore."

There was another pause, a long one. Gosling stared off into the distance. It seemed as if his mind, creaky with age, needed time to conjure up the memories that resided inside.

"Our shared friend Whitfield told me that you'd like to learn more about the Troll, is that right?"

"That's right. If it's not asking too much."

"No bother, no bother at all. Like I said, the Troll was a freak, even at birth. But his parents, the good souls that they were, loved him just the same. Others weren't so kind."

"How do you know this?"

"It wasn't easy to find out. No. It seemed he made every effort to hide his background, to erase what is known about him. I can't tell you why, but he preferred to be something of a mystery. But even a man as clever as the Troll can't stay hidden, not if you have enough means to uncover his secrets. And my resources are nearly unlimited."

There is no proper way to knowledge such a statement. *Good for you,* I could have said, although that would be peculiar. So I said nothing, and Gosling continued.

"Not that I know much. I've never met anyone who's actually seen the Troll. Everything I am about to tell is secondhand, pieced together like the child's game of telephone. But here's what I do know."

He let out a long sigh.

"The Troll came into this world the same way as you and me. But it was immediately obvious that he was different. In kindergarten, the other normal kids teased him relentlessly, made fun of his long nose and odd skin. But that changed around the fourth grade, because by then the Troll was already six-feet tall, even the eighth-grade bullies left him alone. By his first year of high school he was close to seven feet tall. The basketball coach recruited him for the varsity team. The Troll had no real skills to speak of, but since he was so big they just threw the ball to him under the basket and he couldn't be stopped. At first, the Troll enjoyed playing ball, being part of a team. But that only lasted a few games, and then he quit. Sports weren't his thing. He loved science and learning and he adored computers. In that way he's not unlike me. Or you."

Gosling looked at me in a way that led me to believe he knew quite a bit about my background as well.

"Throughout high school the Troll kept to himself," Gosling said. "When he wasn't in class you could often find him in the library. He was a prolific reader. Philosophy, politics, and history – they all attracted his attention. But what he was most interested in was science, physics in particular. And the area of physics that he found most interesting was quantum mechanics." Gosling paused for a moment, looked me in the eye. "Do you know what quantum mechanics is?"

I was forced to admit that I didn't.

"It's the study of microscopic materials, things that are orders of magnitude smaller than atoms. I'm not an expert myself, but as I understand it, particles at the quantum mechanics level don't behave in the same way as large material does. There isn't necessarily a direct cause-and-effect. Instead, behavior is defined by probabilities. And how an item behaves can be impacted by how it's observed and measured. Are you following?"

I nodded, although in truth it had flown over my head.

"In the school library, the Troll would squeeze his enormous frame into the chairs that were built for regular-sized people. Since he was so mountainous it looked like he needed to be shoehorned into his seat. A yellow pencil was typically tucked behind one ear, a cluttered notepad on the floor. He would take notes on things that captured his interest. When he wasn't reading, more often than not, he could be found in the school's computer room. His hands were too big for the keyboards, so he had to peck with his index fingers. He came across as anti-social, a loner."

"Was he lonely?" I injected.

"Maybe, but who can say? I'm not willing to impose traditional emotional needs on him. He's different than you and I. In many ways, he's superior."

We finished off what was left of our drinks. The sun had dipped under the trees and the air cooled noticeably, although not enough to force us to move inside. I slouched down in my chair.

Gosling continued with his story.

"Still, the Troll had no friends. And after his junior year, he dropped out of school. The ensuing decades are a blank. I have no concrete details on what he did. It's like he simply vanished. Of course, there are rumors, all related to the government. One is that he was recruited by the CIA. Another that he joined the Pentagon, part of a special ops team. A third that he was put in charge of the search for alien life. And still another that he was he made a personal assistant to a line of presidents – a sort of jack-of-all trades who could be moved from assignment to assignment."

Gosling spread some cheese on a cracker and ate it. Priya had left a pitcher of water and two glasses. We filled our glasses and drank.

"Which rumor do you believe?" I asked.

"None of them. All of them. Or maybe somewhere in between. In the end it doesn't matter what I believe. But what is clear is that at some point the Troll moved beyond just studying theoretical physics, and began to put some of what he'd learned into practice."

He fell into silence. The two of us entered a long, dark tunnel. The tunnel continued for nearly three minutes. Or maybe it wasn't a tunnel at all. Perhaps Gosling, who had clamped his eyes shut, had just drifted off into sleep. I didn't say a word, unwilling to break the spell. I tried to picture the Troll in a basketball uniform, a tank top, little shorts, and canvas high tops.

Eventually Gosling snapped himself out of his reverie and said, "I had never heard of the Troll until one day when I was given a presentation by the founders of Centre Terrain. They'd arranged a meeting with me, they wanted to pitch me on their company, see if I'd be willing to invest. I frankly thought it was unlikely but I was interested enough to agree to a meeting. I listened politely to the first two presenters, although what they said didn't interest me. Then a third man spoke. He explained the processor, the flexible integrated circuit, and how it would connect directly to the brain. He detailed why it was needed, that without such a device it wasn't possible to repair the tears in the program, at least not as rapidly as required. He didn't completely open the kimono, but he provided enough technical information to make it compelling. To say I was intrigued would be a wild understatement. But like I said earlier, I didn't think it would work. I *still* don't think it should work."

He cleared his throat again.

"I asked them how the processor was created, who developed it. They gave me a two-word response."

"The Troll," I said.

"Yes, the Troll. But when I asked if I could meet him I was told that was impossible. I was informed that not one of them had ever met the Troll, at least not directly. All communication was handled electronically. 'He's something of a Howard Hughes-type,' one of the founders told me. But I went ahead and wrote a check. Why not? I was intrigued and I could afford to lose the money. And the rest of the story, as they say, is history. The company took off. The processor apparently works. But I never did get to meet the Troll."

≈≈≈

The air cooled even further and I wished I hadn't left my jacket in the car. A humming bird flitted among the flowerpots, its wings flapping as fast as a heartbeat.

Gosling shifted in his chair. "I've grown tired," he said. "One of the many handicaps of old age is sudden weariness. You asked to learn more about the Troll, and I hope I helped. I hope the ramblings of an old man weren't too much to handle."

As I looked on, Gosling floated off to sleep.

≈≈≈

It was around six in the evening when I returned to the front of the house where the robotic car awaited. Priya had walked with me, and I thanked her for all her help.

"My pleasure," she said.

For the first time that day she smiled, slightly, and it hit me how attractive she was. How could I have missed it until that moment? Maybe I had overlooked her appeal because of her height? There is a particular body type that I'm normally attracted to – petite, yet curvy – and Priya was neither. She was sporty and statuesque. Still, despite the fact that she didn't fit my ideal, I found myself suddenly aroused, in a skin-prickling sort of way.

I chuckled to myself. The previous night I had slept with a woman for the first time in years, and here I was scoping out someone else.

Then I caught a whiff of Priya's perfume. The smell floored me. It was like being visited by an old friend. You see, it was the same perfume that was worn by Nika. And the thing is I had *never* met another woman who wore that same scent. I found its appearance at that point so remarkable that I questioned whether it was real. Thoughts like that sometimes occur to me. That what I believed I was experiencing was in truth only something that I'd conjured up. But then again, what is reality, except what lives in our minds?

It was just perfume, anyway. Not a big deal. Maybe it was the latest hot brand and Priya and Nika were early adopters?

"Would it be okay if we kept in touch?" Priya asked. The smile had slipped away and her face had resumed its normal composed expression.

"Absolutely, call me whenever you want."

"Mr. Gosling may have not communicated it, but I know he'd be eager to learn more about the Troll as well."

"I'll tell you what I'll do. If I learn anything more I'll call you right away."

"Splendid. Now is there anything else I can do for you?"

"Actually, there is. Is it possible to change the soundtrack for the ride home?" I pointed toward the car. "That Muzak killed me."

"Sure. What would you like?"

"How about just the radio, KFOG?"

"Done."

17

My phone rang on the drive back to San Francisco and I answered it without checking caller ID, a decision I immediately regretted.

"You missed our practice session today." It was Edzard. He sounded cranky. I could picture smoke steaming out of his ears, like in a Warner Brothers cartoon.

It slipped my mind, I told him.

He asked how the presentation was coming.

It's moving along, I lied. I hadn't dedicated a single second to developing it.

When can I see it?

I told him it needed a little fine-tuning.

Email me what you got, he snapped.

I will, I will, just not yet.

He breathed heavily into the phone. It was so loud I had to pull the receiver away from my ear. He told me I was walking on thin ice. "You're walking on thin ice," he said, using those exact words. The line went dead. The bastard had hung up without saying goodbye.

Whatever...

The highway was nearly empty. The car drove so fast and silently and smoothly it felt like riding on a monorail. It was dusk and the sunlight had ebbed, softened. But I could still make out a thick wall of fog as it climbed over the top of the Santa Cruz Mountains. Although it tried to gallop downhill, it wasn't strong enough to survive the inland heat and dissolved.

I thought about the Troll and replayed what Gosling had told me. His story was both odd and mundane at the same time. *We're going to change the world*, the Troll had said. What did he mean? No answers presented themselves, my mind a desert.

On the radio "Trojans" by *Atlas Genius* – my song – started to play. It wasn't a wildly popular tune, so I found its appearance at the moment somewhat interesting. Although it does seem like the universe works that way at times, gives me what I'm asking for. My eyes felt like lead. They dropped shut. I shook myself awake – once, twice – but after a few minutes gave in and drifted off to sleep.

I dreamt that I was a student back at Stanford. In my dream I was fast asleep, a coma-like slumber, and as a result I was late for a final exam. It was a cruel, reoccurring nightmare, but this time with a twist. A dwarf shook me awake.

"Who are you," I asked. I was awake in my dream, but still asleep in real life.

"The Dwarf." He had a long beard and a face so weathered it looked like it had suffered through a century of icy winters.

"Heigh-Ho?" I asked.

"Don't be ridiculous."

"Do you need help killing the dragon Smaug?"

"You read too many fairytales."

"Well, what the hell are you doing here?"

"You were visited by a troll. Why not dream about a dwarf?"

I couldn't argue with that logic.

"Wait!" I said, "I need to get to a final exam!"

"That's right, college boy, get your ass out of bed and let's move!"

The Dwarf tugged my pajama sleeve and dragged me out of bed. The next thing I knew I was in a classroom – no walking, I just appeared there. I was still wearing my pajamas. The teacher – I'd never seen him before. Classmates – they were strangers, every one of 'em. I was handed an exam. The text was written in an indecipherable argot. It made as much sense to me as a book written in Klingon. My skin turned cold. I was gripped with a paralyzing sensation, an oppressive feeling of doom that I would fail this test and as a result my life would be ruined.

I woke in jolt. It took me a moment, but I gathered myself and then I checked my text messages. There was a note from Nika.

Let's meet for dinner tonight at Foreign Cinema. 7:30. Okay?

I sent a note back: *On my way.*

18

In reality, I never did take a final exam at Stanford, not a single one. Dropping out of school was easy, no paperwork required, the Captain and I just stopped going to class. Since we'd paid our tuition for the semester we could've stayed in the dorms, but decided that wasn't the way to launch a company. So we rented a cozy one-story house in a high rent neighborhood just off campus. Of course, every neighborhood in Palo Alto was high rent. The town was drenched in money. The house was just a few blocks from where Steve Jobs lived, which I thought was cool.

We stopped going to movies. We didn't eat out. No more video games or visits to the gym, there wasn't even time to grab a beer at the local watering hole. Our lives revolved around making Polpo a success. For months, I spent every day feverishly working to refine the audience measurement program that I'd shown the Captain. We both knew we'd be late to market, so our only chance for success was to build a better product.

It seemed a positive omen that on the first day of spring – March twenty-one – one of the VC meetings paid off and we got our first round of funding. The windows of the house were cracked, a cool breeze seeped in. I'd slept in and stood at the stove, scrambling eggs. I still wore my robe and slippers.

The back door opened. In walked the Captain, dressed in a sweatshirt and blue jeans. He sported a shit-eating grin.

"We're in business," he said. He held up a green check between his fingers. I peered at it. Series A funding: $3 million. Not outrageous, as these things go, but not chump change either.

"Is this for real?" I asked.

"As a heart attack."

We moved shop to a small building on University Avenue. It was a basement, but nice enough. It felt good to have a real office for a change. We hired a skeleton crew, exclusively young people willing to work insane hours for a promise of riches. Each night we brought in food – pizza, Chinese – so everyone could continue working through the dinner hour and beyond. It was all standard start-up stuff.

I took the title: Head Geek. The Captain anointed himself CEO.

"We're not focused on revenue," he told me, "at least not yet."

"You don't say."

"Of course not. It's start-up one-oh-one. Build a customer base and then monetize it."

"Okay..."

I didn't fully process what he had told me. The Captain handled the business side, employees, finance: all the non-techy stuff. I lived inside the code, to the point where I wasn't clear where it started and I ended. I polished the program with lapidary care, made it perfect, and then went back and perfected it some more.

The Captain took a bite of pizza and washed it down with a sip of Coke. "We're doing it, my friend. We're really going make this happen."

Soon Series B funding came through, more millions. We moved to San Francisco. We hired more people. The years flew by in a blur. I believed my shoes could have made the walk from my apartment to the office on their own, it seemed like those were the only two places I went.

Still, I loved it. I felt inspired and challenged by what we were trying to accomplish. But something, no doubt, was lost. Was there a Presidential election one of those years? Who won the Super Bowl? Sex – forget it. I'd shut down that side of me. I even stopped dreaming.

But one day the crazy ride came to an end. And somehow my whole Polpo experience was connected to the Troll, maybe not in a big way, perhaps they were just two pieces in a large puzzle, but they were tied together. I couldn't say exactly how I came to that conclusion – call it a sixth sense – but I was sure that it was true.

I arrived at the restaurant at a little after 7:30. Nika was inside, seated at the front bar, already partway through a glass of wine. It was Sauvignon blanc, by the looks of it. Foreign Cinema had two bars, a small dining room, and a larger room where black-and-white silent movies were broadcast on the tall brick walls. You could watch a Charlie Chaplin flick while you ate California-influenced Mediterranean-style cuisine. It was ultra-chic, one of the first posh restaurants to pop up in the Mission, back during the Dot Com craze, when the area began its gentrification.

I asked the bartender to bring me a Bloody Mary, and he rounded up two menus. Nika ordered seafood pasta. Since I was still full from eating at Gosling's I just got a small salad.

When the food arrived we each ordered another drink. It was my fifth cocktail of the day, and although they'd been spread out over a few hours and separated by a nap, I was feeling decidedly groggy. The conversation was light as we ate our dinners – that is until Nika said something that practically caused me to choke on a cherry tomato.

"So what did Gosling tell you about the Troll?"

I started to cough, so violently that I took my napkin off my lap and covered my mouth. "Excuse me," I said, once the fit had ended. You see, I'd never told Nika about either Gosling or the Troll.

"That's where you've been this afternoon, right, at Gosling's?" She pushed the food around her plate with her fork. Her expression looked as placid as if she's asked me to give her my recipe for potato soup.

"And how, exactly, did you know that?" I immediately jumped to the conclusion that she was either monitoring my online activities, or had hired a private eye to keep tabs on me.

She crinkled her eyebrows and smiled enigmatically. "Now don't get huffy. I haven't had you followed," she said, as if reading my mind. "I shouldn't have just sprung the question on you, huh?"

I ignored her question and went with one of my own. "So how did you know?" It occurred to me that she might have heard my morning phone conversation with Priya. Nika had been, after all, lying next to me. Perhaps she hadn't really been asleep?

She didn't answer, but instead poked at her food some more. I took a sip of my Bloody Mary. Eventually I prodded her: "So how *did* you know?" I repeated for a third time.

She diverted her eyes, shifted uncomfortably in her chair. She seemed hesitant to respond, but eventually said, "I just know. I don't want to get into how I know, I just do."

The room seemed to move, or maybe the earth itself shifted, broke free of its axis. I was gripped with an unsettling sensation that I was someone else. I grabbed my cocktail, took a big drink, before I finally mustered up a response. "Okay."

Less than twenty-four hours earlier, Nika and I had engaged in multiple carnal acts that had rocked my world. But as I sat at the bar I became gripped with a feeling that it had all been a ruse, a ploy to get close to me and learn more about the Troll.

I wanted to leave and process what I'd just learned.

Luckily, I had a ready-made escape hatch. "Look," I

said, "I'm sorry, but I need to cut things short. Edzard is on my ass to complete a presentation for tomorrow's developer's conference, and I haven't even started it yet." This had the added benefit of being the truth. "Let's discuss this later, okay?"

Nika finished her glass of wine and said, "Okay. But come with me first."

≈≈≈

Nika took my hand and pulled me toward the bathroom. She walked briskly and I worked to keep up, caught in a trail of perfume. For a moment I pictured Priya – smart outfit, velvety hair.

Once inside, Nika locked the door. The bathroom was one of those high-end jobs with just one toilet and walls painted a stylized dark green, a type of green I'm not sure exists in nature. There were framed watercolors on the walls and a glass bowl next to the sink that was full of spectacularly colorful and pungent potpourri. The room was spacious. That bathroom was nicer than some San Francisco apartments I'd visited.

Without speaking, Nika placed her hand on my crotch and rubbed. I felt myself stiffen. Her lips brushed mine, gently, almost imperceptivity. She gave off an air of brooding sensuality. With animal-like dexterity, her fingers clutched my belt buckle and she pulled me along as she eased backward until her back was pressed against a wall. With one graceful motion she reached a hand under her skirt and stepped out of her panties. Then she unbuckled my pants, slid the zipper down. I pushed her against the wall, her legs bent like a frog's and we fucked. Her eyes rolled up into her head and she arched her back and pressed herself against me. It was angry and lascivious.

Damn. It was hot.

So maybe she was using me, and maybe that made me

feel a little uneasy, and maybe it was possible that she'd slept with me just so she could learn more about the Troll, but at that moment I just didn't care. Hell, if it were possible, I'd have let her unscrew the top of my skull and dig around until she uncovered every bit of information on the Troll that was locked up inside.

20

The hardware store was tucked along a narrow street in a quaint little village, a town that had all the trappings of an upscale East Coast community. There was an old-time barbershop, ice cream parlor, a bicycle store. Why would a coder want to re-create something that existed in the real world? It seemed so unimaginative, but all the same, Roma was glad that he'd found it.

Roma plucked a caliper – a device used to measure the size of an object – off a shelf, took it to the front of the store, and tried to pay for it. But the servile clerk manning the cash register insisted he take it free of charge.

"Please," the clerk said, "I would be honored if you accepted it as a gift. I insist."

Whatever rocks his boat, Roma thought.

With the caliper in hand, Roma zipped directly to the mushroom field. More mushrooms had sprouted, they were packed in thick. Using his newly acquired tool, Roma measured the portal. It was exactly five millimeters in diameter. Okay, easy enough to remember. With that done, Roma tucked the device into the inside pocket of his vest, opened a pop-up window, got down to work.

He coded. His fingers started fast, picked up speed, a ball bouncing down a staircase. Roma's mind was filled with only the absence of thought. Space seemed to expand around him. Butterflies frantically circled. The sea of mushrooms that spread out all around grew noticeably. They climbed upward. Roma didn't just program, he *was* programming.

And then – in time – he stopped. Roma re-measured the hole, groaned. You've got to be kidding me. The portal had grown one-tenth of a millimeter.

All that work and that was it: One. Fucking. Tenth.

Discouraged, Roma was about to leave, to seek refuge in the outside world, when he spied the big-eyed Halfling. The Halfling stood next to a tall, purple mushroom. Roma was overcome by a feeling of communion. Was it one-sided? The Halfling didn't speak. He cocked his head to one side, smiled knowingly.

21

Less than an hour after leaving Nika and I arrived at my apartment. I logged onto my laptop. On the cab ride from the restaurant Edzard had sent me three texts, each ensuing message more shrill than the previous one, all demanding an update on the presentation. I ignored them. But I knew I *had* to get the presentation done. So I opened a PowerPoint template, wrote a title page and a table of contents slide. Then I got bored. The presentation needed to be developed – it was an inescapable truth, like gravity. But it didn't need to be completed yet, no, not just yet. There was still time. Or so I figured. I closed the application.

I rolled a joint, a real fatty, and smoked it until my head was a foggy mess. Then I walked to the refrigerator and snatched a bottle of Anchor Steam. Why stop the drinking at that point? Besides, although I hadn't written a lot of presentations – any, really – how hard could it be? I'd seen the Captain give hundreds of them. He was a pro. Surely I'd picked up something through osmosis. Banging one out should be a snap.

Then something bit my toe.

I looked down and saw Magnus Carlsen. He hadn't clamped down strongly enough to inflict real pain, but with just enough force to get my attention. He meowed, took a few steps to the bedroom. When he saw I wasn't following he meowed again, loudly.

"Sorry, bro," I said, "I'll have to join you later."

I watched as he leapt up onto the bed and nestled into

the duvet. I was depleted, cashed, and nothing would have made me happier than to join Magnus, get some shuteye. But I had to finish the damn presentation. Time was slipping away, fast. Two more texts from Edzard arrived. The second one read – *I hope for your sake you're in a hospital. Or dead. And if I don't hear from you soon, we're going to cut your spot.*

I couldn't blame him for being pissed. Centre Terrain Open World was a big deal. Thousands of people attended. I assumed all of the other presentations were already in the can. And I was presenting on the opening day, right after the CEO, which was just hours away. It was a prime spot. If my presentation bombed – or worse, I had nothing to show – it would reflect poorly on Edzard for assigning me the task.

So I opened the PowerPoint I'd barely started earlier determined to get back to work. Unfortunately, I was immediately confronted by a wall of boredom. The deck just felt wrong. It was tedious, needed some pizzazz. In an effort to find some inspiration, I sparked the joint I'd rolled earlier in the evening. I worked it pretty good, got three decent sized hits. And shockingly, the ploy paid off – I was hit with an inspiration. Why finish a banal slide deck when I could make a video instead? PowerPoint is dull; videos are fun, and definitely more in my wheelhouse. So that's what I did, I cut a video. It was just a few minutes long, but informative, funny, entertaining.

I sent Edzard a text that read: *It's done. I'll see you tomorrow. You're going to like what you see!*

When I finally climbed into bed Magnus was so out of it that he barely stirred. I was so tired that I didn't even check the time. As soon as my head hit the pillow I passed out.

22

It was four days since I'd seen the Troll. I hadn't heard from him again. Would I? Was it just a vivid dream? No, it was real, I knew that much.

I stepped inside one of the ubiquitous boutique coffee shops that are sprinkled throughout the city and ordered an enormous latte. The paper cup was half the size of my forearm, a young child might drown inside it. As I walked along Third Avenue toward the Moscone Center I thought again about the Troll's words: *We're going to change the world.*

But there was no time to properly ponder their meaning. I needed to shift my focus onto my upcoming presentation.

Howard Street, which bisects the two Moscone buildings (officially named the North and South halls), was closed to car traffic. An enormous blue tent was stretched across the street, and a battalion-sized throng of convention goers sampled from the different food courts scattered underneath.

In addition to being a developer conference, Centre Terrain Open World was also a user convention, loosely patterned after Comic Con. Gamers were encouraged to dress up like their avatars.

The costumes could get very elaborate, and as I squeezed my way through the crowd I was confronted by an endless procession of Orcs, Goblins, Warriors, and

Wizards.

When I finally made it inside the South Hall and down the escalator, I was met backstage by a decidedly peeved Edzard. He looked ready to erupt, but I cut him off before he could say a word.

"Don't worry, chief, I have a presentation."

"These things need to be vetted," he practically shouted. "You can't just show up the day of the show. Why did I trust you?" He paused for a bit and then said, "We decided to cut your presentation."

"No – you can't do that. You're going to like what I have – trust me."

This seemed to calm him, if only mildly. "Let's at least take a quick look at the slides."

"Slides, well, here's the thing. There are no slides. I cut a video."

He didn't say a word, but his face turned as red as a tomato. I thought he might cry. He was in the midst of an existential crisis. I could see him calculating: was it riskier, at this late date, for him to yank me from the program or let me showcase my unvetted video?

I didn't wait for him to come to a resolution. The company's CEO, who was currently onstage, had only a few minutes left on his keynote address. I broke away, left Edzard to cool his heels, found the head of the show's production group, gave him a CD on which I'd burned a copy of my video, instructed him to cue it up. It would be unthinkable to run a previously unseen video at a major trade show sponsored by one of the more buttoned-down companies in the Valley. But Centre Terrain had such a loosey-goosey approach to marketing that I knew I could slip it in.

≈≈≈

On the official agenda, my presentation was entitled: *Tips on Creating Apps*. There were over ten thousand people in the audience waiting to hear me speak. They were seated in folding chairs that stretched out from the foot of the elevated stage all the way to the back of the hall. As I waited off to the side, the show's MC gave me a brief introduction and then asked me to join him. There was polite applause when I made my entrance. The MC and I sat down on extra-tall stools set in the middle of the stage. Between us was a tall, round table which held two bottles of water. We sipped from the bottles and had an unscripted discussion covering various elements of programming: which apps I'd found most useful, ideas on how best to monetize a particular creation – that sort of thing.

After about fifteen minutes the MC said, "So I understand you have a video for us to watch."

"That's right."

"Well, let's go ahead and run it."

The lights were lowered and the room went nearly black. Behind us was an enormous monitor, perhaps forty-feet long. When my video started I was struck by how good the production quality appeared, especially since I'd created it in the middle of the night, and half-in-the-bag.

My digital face took up the entire screen. I was seated at my desk, in my apartment, talking directly into the camera placed on top of my laptop. My eyes were a little bloodshot, but otherwise it was impossible to tell I was stoned. Or at least so I thought. I spoke for just a minute or two, motherhood and apple stuff about the importance of our third-party developer community. And then I said, "Now I want to give you a little demonstration on the best way to navigate through the program. Better yet – let's let my friend give the demonstration."

As the camera rolled, I put on my augmentation glasses, the world of Centre Terrain formed around me, and I morphed into Roma. The audience hooted, whistled, and applauded. The adulation equaled what I'd expect to hear at a Star Trek convention if Leonard Nimoy had made an unplanned appearance. It was cool, uplifting. On the big screen above me, Roma opened a pop-up window and ran through a series of programming tips. Because of the noise that emanated from the cheering it was actually a little difficult to hear what Roma said. But it didn't matter. It was theater, and the crowd ate it up.

≈≈≈

I felt giddy from the crowd's adulation, and when my portion of the event ended I practically floated backstage. But Edzard, who was waiting for me in the wings, promptly squashed my good mood.

"What the fuck was that?" he asked, as he pressed his face close to mine. The blood vessels at the base of his nose were engorged, so much so that I feared one might burst.

"I thought it went well." I tried to walk around him, but he took a step to the side and blocked my path.

"*Well*? You gave away your identity. Everyone now knows that you're Roma."

Whoops. He was right, I had done that. Such an act was more than just frowned upon, it was strictly against company policy, and its importance was routinely and shrilly pounded home to every Sweeper.

"It slipped my mind," I said, honestly.

"Impossible. I should fire you right now. The Sweeper anonymity policy is one that – "

"We should seriously consider doing away with," said a high male voice, cutting Edzard off in mid-sentence. It was the company's CEO. He stepped into the space that Edzard and I had been sharing. "Can you hear that crowd?" The CEO put the question to Edzard. "They love it. We have a rock star on our hands." He glanced my way and then back toward Edzard. "I think we should create a marketing campaign that identifies who all of our

Sweepers are, a gimmick. Drum up a little excitement."

"That could cause problems," said Edzard, "we can't –"

"We can and we will. Why didn't you think of this?"

The CEO hadn't been part of the original company founders, but was brought in from the outside when it was deemed by Centre Terrain's board of directors that the company had grown so large it needed adult supervision. He had a long ponytail and round, rimless pince-nez glasses that I'm sure were selected to bestow on him an air of intellectual superiority. His management style was characterized by making rash, ad hoc decisions, an approach that I'd thought had marked him as an empty suit.

I'd always thought he was a pompous ass, a perfect blend of unbending arrogance and supreme incompetence. But at that particular moment I found myself happy that he'd appeared.

The CEO looked at me and said, "Great job." His eyes zeroed in on my face. "You look exhausted. Why don't you call it a day, go home and get some sleep."

That sounded like exactly what I needed. "Thanks – I'll do that."

Right before I stepped out the back exit, I looked backward and saw Edzard's pained expression as he listened to the CEO pontificate.

23

Despite the fact that I was completely wiped out, my time on stage and the reaction from the crowd had gotten my adrenaline pumping so rapidly that it made sleep impossible. So, once back in my apartment, instead of climbing into bed for a midday nap, I logged back into Centre Terrain.

≈≈≈

The mushrooms were still there – dense, fragrant – and the butterflies too. Roma opened a pop-up window and got down to business. After an hour or so he measured the hole. It had grown by two-tenths of a millimeter.

Damn.

His inability to pry open the hole touched him with a kind of panic. Were his skills eroding? He leaned toward the offending circle, peered inside, took in the wispy fog on the other side. *One-tenth before, two-tenths now, so slow,* he thought.

"Not slow. Fast. *Hmmmaaa...*" said a voice. The voice belonged to the Halfling, of course, the weird and familiar Halfling. His eyes, if possible, looked even larger than before. Roma made a mental note to look for him the next time.

"What are you talking about?" Roma asked. "That's practically nothing."

"No. No. At this rate it will soon be large enough for you to step through. *Hmmmaaa...*"

Roma contemplated arguing with him, but he didn't see the point. So he just said, "Whatever," and exited the game.

≈≈≈

After freshening up Magnus' milk bowl, I shut all the curtains in my apartment and climbed into bed.

24

I was in a deep sleep and enjoying a dream that featured me and Nika and my former lover from the golf course, all engaged in a variety of sultry activities – the threesome, every man's fantasy – when, to my annoyance, my cell phone rang. But my mood brightened when I checked the display and saw it was Priya on the other end.

"I'm sorry. Did I wake you?" she asked.

"No," I lied, "I've been up." I glanced at my phone, which read just past five, meaning I'd been asleep for at least four hours.

"Good. I wanted to follow up on your discussion with Mr. Gosling. Did you get what you needed?"

She was efficient to a fault. "Yes, it was very helpful. Thank you."

The conversation lapsed. I thought that was the end of it, but then she said, "I heard you put on quite a show this morning. At Moscone."

"News travels fast."

"Apparently you made a big impression. So you're this Roma character?"

"Uh-huh."

"How does that feel?"

"Amazing. The game itself is a blast, but what I can do with my character is something else altogether."

"I see."

"Do you play?"

"Oh – no. I couldn't see myself doing something like that. It's a little ironic, considering I work for Mr. Gosling, but I'm really a bit of a Luddite. If you can believe it, I just got my first cell phone this year. And it isn't even a smartphone, just an old style flip. I can make phone calls and send text messages, but that's the extent of it."

I did have trouble believing it. I knew that there existed people like Priya – late adopters, or individuals who eschewed technology altogether – but I hadn't met any of them personally. In the circles I ran in, everyone was eager to get the latest smartphone or tablet or whatever whizzy new gadget had hit the market.

"I think you're missing out," I said. "The iPhone is amazing."

"Maybe you can help me buy one?"

"Yeah. Sure."

"We could make an outing out of it. We could meet in the city and you can help me buy an iPhone, and then we can get lunch. How does that sound?"

How does that sound? I repeated what she'd said in my head. I didn't respond right away, and in the silence I might have injected more meaning into her suggestion than it warranted.

During my short stay at Stanford, there was a sophomore on my dorm floor, Jimmy, who had a catch phrase. Whenever one of the guys would mention an innocuous comment that a woman at school had said – that she liked his coat or was considering taking the same class he was in or whatever – Jimmy would say, "You know why she said that, right?" The reply would come, "No. Why?" And Jimmy would answer, "Because she wants to *fuck* you." This line, although at some point predictable, never failed to illicit a laugh. The laughter was a result both of the punch line's absurdity, and because in truth, buried deep inside each man's head, that is the very question we ponder (oh, if women only knew the whole truth).

So was it possible – I wondered – if two beautiful women were interested in sleeping with me, first Nika and now Priya?

"Are you still there?" she asked, jogging me out of my thoughts.

"Yeah. Yes, yes. iPhone and lunch, that sounds good," I said.

"Wonderful. I'll put together an itinerary and get back to you."

An itinerary: she was efficient to a fault.

≈≈≈

After the line went dead, I almost put the phone down, but then it started to ring again. Whitfield.

"Keemo," he said, "did Gosling get in touch with you?"

I told him that he had, and that I'd already met with him

"Outstanding. I want to hear all about it. I'm walking into Bix now. Come join me for a drink."

"Give me thirty minutes."

Next I sent Nika a text: *Are you free tonight? Ciao.* Although I felt weird about our conversation the night before, I still wanted to see her.

A reply arrived a minute later: *Tonight. Call me. xxoo.*

25

Inside Bix I searched for Whitfield until I found him in a booth in the corner of the room. A waitress was removing an empty martini glass and depositing a full one in front of him. By the glassy look in his eyes I guessed it was probably his third.

The room had just a smattering of patrons – it was only Monday, after all – mostly men wearing suits and ties, pressed up against the bar. A piano player near the entrance played Cole Porter standards: "I've Got You Under My Skin"; "I Get a Kick Out of You."

Whitfield had heard about my video presentation from that morning, and we spent some time discussing it, and Edzard's reaction, and the timely rescue from Centre Terrain's CEO. Afterward Whitfield asked how the meeting went with Gosling.

"Good, I guess, I learned a lot."

"About the Troll, you mean?"

"That's right – the Troll."

"Such as..."

I recapped what Gosling had told me. Whitfield listened. A few times he nodded his head and said, "Good, good – interesting." When I'd finished, he ate the two olives that had been soaking in his drink, looked at me sideways, and asked why I appeared so glum. "You look like someone has stolen your girl."

"Maybe in a way, someone has."

"Don't you first have to have a girl to lose one?"

"That's right, I haven't told you. Things have been

moving kind of fast for me lately. But I met someone. Or actually, I've known her – Nika – but we just started dating. Or at least we've had one official date."

"Bravo. So what's she like?"

I described her.

"She sounds a little kooky, but that's good. The best one's always are. And how's the sex?"

"What makes you think we've had sex?"

"Come on – with that puppy dog face? No man can be that messed up by a woman unless he's screwed her. I'm right, am I not?"

I hemmed and hawed, but then acknowledged that we had slept together.

I even found myself providing details on our encounter in the bathroom. As Whitfield took in that story, he started to nod his head. I followed suit, until both our noggins were bouncing up and down like a couple of bobblehead dolls.

"That's hot," he said, "so why so sad? What's the problem?"

"Well, I think that there's a good chance that she's with me just because she wants to learn more about the Troll."

"What do you mean?"

I told him about our discussion the previous night at Foreign Cinema.

He let what he learned sink in for a moment, before saying, "Okay – so what if that's true? I can imagine a lot of people would be interested in learning more about the Troll. And besides, porn star sex like what you've described comes along only a few times in your life. You need to ride that as long as possible – pun fully intended."

"You think so?"

"Absolutely. No offense, but it's not like you're a player."

"True," I acknowledged, begrudgingly.

He bent his head to one side. "So what are you doing here with me? You should be at home right now having a booty call."

He was right, I realized. But it helped to have Whitfield there to point out the obvious. So we asked the waiter for the bill, each paid our share, and I was out the door.

≈≈≈

Once outside I immediately called Nika, speed dial. She answered right away.

"You've been a naughty boy," she said.

"How do you mean?"

"That stunt you pulled today at the developer conference. Come on! What were you thinking?"

I mumbled something incoherent into the receiver.

"Not that I didn't enjoy it. It was great. I would have loved to see the expression on Edzard's face."

"It wasn't too different from the day you had Jett kill that army of Orcs."

She laughed. "Yeah, he was pissed."

"So what happened?"

"Nothing really. Just a stern warning and a promise that I'd never do it again. I'm sure you'll get the same treatment."

"Changing subjects," I said. "Want to get together tonight?"

"Uh-huh."

"Want to meet me at my place?"

"No. Let's go to a party."

"Party..."

"A party, yeah, although it's really more of an event. It's happening in the Mission. Come on, it'll be fun."

"All right, I'm game."

She offered to get a cab and pick me up. I gave her my

location, and not long after she arrived.

≈≈≈

"So we're going to a place called HUB," Nika told me in the backseat of the cab.

We held hands and the car steered onto Valencia Street into what was still a hardscrabble part of the Mission District, but was also showing some signs of revitalization. The city was in the process of undergoing a steady re-gentrification, financed by the tidal wave of money flowing in from the tech industry. I was ambivalent about it. There was no doubt that I appreciated a little sprucing up, but at what cost? Artists and teachers and city workers and so many others found it increasingly difficult to fork over the ridiculous and still rising rents, to actually live in the place where they worked. San Francisco ran the risk of being a one-industry town, and in the process losing part of its appeal, its character.

"HUB?" I asked.

"It's a collective, strictly non-profit. Its goal is to bring together people from the arts and technology, and..." here she made air quotes, "...push culture forward."

That sounded like a rather audacious goal. I pictured a group of people in their twenties drinking beer, mingling, and acting self-important.

Nika must have caught the skeptical look on my face because she let go of my hand and gave me a gentle punch on the deltoid. "Don't be a curmudgeon. Every month they have an event, and tonight there's a speaker from Twitter. He'll be followed by a local band. Come on, it's cool, we'll have fun."

≈≈≈

The building where HUB resided had clearly once been a firehouse. It had been renovated to look like an art gallery, although there was still a fire pole – just for decoration – which ran from floor to ceiling in the back corner. On the walls were hung large and eye-catching paintings. I'm not an art expert, but they all seemed to give off an aesthetic vibe that was inspired in equal parts by the commercial commentary of some of Andy Warhol's work, and the abstract expressionism of Jackson Pollock. It was a funky mixture, but it worked.

"Everything here was created by local artists," Nika told me, as we passed a large canvas near the front entrance, "people who work and live in San Francisco."

There was only the one room, which was large and jammed with people who sat cross-legged on the floor and looked at a small stage in the far corner, right near the fire pole. The audience wasn't far off from what I'd imagined in the cab. Everyone was under thirty and dressed casually; they were hip, but in a nerdy, brainy way.

"Let's take a seat," Nika said. "It looks like the show is about to start."

The speaker from Twitter stepped onto the stage. His talk, however, didn't focus on the company. Instead, he spent his allocated time discussing privacy on the Internet. I found it dull. It's not that I don't care about privacy, it's just that long ago I accepted Scott McNealy's mantra: *You have zero privacy anyway. Get over it.*

As the Twitter guy wrapped up, a different dude stood up from the legs-crossed crowd and walked past where Nika and I were. She stood as well, tugged me to follow, and we chased after the man.

"Crandall," she said, and he stopped, turned to face us.

He wore a Sherlock Holmes-style hat and a blue t-shirt with a Jesus fish on the front. But instead of saying "Jesus" the fish was emblazoned with the word "Darwin."

"I wanted the two of you to meet." Nika introduced us and we shook hands. "Crandall is one of the founders of HUB. And my friend here," she nodded toward me, "is a brilliant programmer."

"Is that so?" Crandall asked. "What do you program?"

"For starters, brilliant is an overstatement. And truthfully, I haven't written a line of code in, God, how long has it been? Over a year, I guess."

This wasn't technically true. Since I'd joined Centre Terrain I'd spent a good deal of time programming, as much as eight hours a day fixing bugs. And because of the processor in my head, I was able to work at a much faster rate than I had before. I was improved, a real fiend. But since I did it all as Roma and not my true self – at least to my way of thinking – I discarded it, whether I should have or not.

Nika broke in. "I need to find the ladies room. You two go on talking."

"So you're taking a break," Crandall said, as Nika worked her way through the crowd. "That's cool. I just got back from two months scuba diving in Australia."

We chewed on the specifics of his trip for a bit, and then the conversation turned toward what Crandall was up to at that moment.

"I have three careers. I'm a seed investor. I've written a couple of books. And I play guitar in a band. Actually, it's my band that's playing tonight."

Investor, writer, and rock star: despite his ridiculous hat, this guy had it going on. I noticed a small tattoo on the inside of his right forearm, three black letters: HUB. "And by seed investor you mean..."

"I give money to fledging tech companies to help them get off the ground. I try to get in early, so the investment is low but the payoff potentially large."

I decided not to push him for any more details, like where did he get the money that allowed him to invest? Had he already had a few successes? Maybe one of his books had done well? Or how did he choose the companies?

A look of recognition crossed his face, like a light bulb

had been turned on. "Hey," Crandall said, "I know you. You were at the developer conference this morning. You're a Sweeper, right? Roma."

Had it just been this morning? It seemed longer ago.

"Yeah, that's right."

"That's cool. I play the game. Add code to the program. The whole works. It must be cool being a Sweeper. You like, have a processor in your head, right, just like Nika?"

I told him I did.

We talked for another five or ten minutes, Crandall wide-eyed, explaining how much he loved the game. His overall attitude shifted, he became jaunty and bright, and I got the feeling he was auditioning, like he was treating our discussion now as if it were a job interview. Although he didn't come right out and say it, it was clear that he wanted to be a Sweeper.

I just nodded, grunted a few responses, but mostly stayed mute. I had zero influence on who Centre Terrain hired. And it was as close to a pure meritocracy as I'd encountered: you either had the programming chops required to handle the job, or you didn't.

Eventually Crandall excused himself so he could go get ready for his gig.

Nika hadn't returned. I wandered around the packed room, narrowed my shoulders so I could squeeze through the sea of people, and gazed at the artwork. I tried to not appear uncomfortable, but I was.

Somehow or other I ended up along a wall with an open door that led outside. I stepped through it and into an alley where a small group of people stood in a loosely formed circle and passed around a blunt. It was quieter out there and I felt immediately more at ease.

I joined the circle of smokers. The guy standing next to me took a hit and then released a river of smoke. He offered me a toke, no questions asked. I took a hit and passed it on. The blunt worked its way around the circle until it landed on me again. I took a second hit, lost track of time. When that blunt was burned to the end someone discarded the dead soldier and sparked up a fresh one. I smoked some more. The sound of Crandall's band floated through the open door. Someone slipped me a cold Heineken and I nursed it and swayed to the rhythm of the music. Not bad. I couldn't tell you how long I'd been outside when I felt a tugging on my sleeve.

"Here you are," said Nika. "You just disappeared. I've been looking for you everywhere!"

"Sorry about that, I just sort of..." and I trailed off.

"No worries. Let's go."

"You want to go inside and listen to the band?"

"No. Home. I found someone who'll give us a ride to my place."

≈≈≈

Nika lived in the basement of a Victorian on Page Street, just a block off Haight. There were bars on the windows. Cement stairs led down to the front door. On the sidewalk near the top of the staircase slept a homeless man. He snored like a freight train. Lying on the ground next to him was a weathered cardboard sign that read, *Need Money to Buy Beer.*

We walked down the stairs and Nika unlocked the front door.

Nika had a studio apartment which was the size of – and I exaggerate just a smidge – a postage stamp. As soon as we stepped inside she led me to her futon bed, which other than a nightstand was the only piece of furniture in the room. She proceeded to yank off my clothes. Nika was definitely the sexually aggressive type. Not that I was complaining. In fact, maybe my personality required the woman to be the assertive one.

We banged out a quickie then propped the pillows up on the headboard and enjoyed the post-coital afterglow. Nika rested her head on my shoulder. We talked for a bit about the party at HUB. She told me she was interested in seed investing.

"It's one of the reasons I moved to San Francisco. This is where all the action is: start-ups, new ideas, innovation. Centre Terrain is just a temporary landing spot. I want to be part of something bigger. I want to create something new, exciting." This seemed to lead naturally to what she said next: "So you still haven't really told me about Gosling and the Troll."

"I haven't?"

"No."

"Well, you still haven't told me how you knew I went to see Gosling. Or how you knew I was visited by the Troll."

Nika lifted herself off me. She sat up on the headboard, pulled the sheet up with her. She released a long sigh and then said, "They popped into my head."

"What popped into your head?"

"Your meeting with Gosling. Your visit from the Troll."

"I'm not following you..."

"Okay. Now I'm going to tell you something, but you first have to promise that you won't label me as some type of mutant."

The past few days had been strange, but apparently it was about to get even stranger.

"Promise?" she repeated

"I promise."

She forced a smile and said, "I'm psychic."

"Excuse me?"

"I'm a psychic," she repeated, and looked me square in the eye.

"Tarot cards, palm readings, crystal ball – that sort of

thing?"

"No." She shook her head. "It's not like that. Things just pop into my mind. Or at least that's how it happens most of the time."

"Things pop into your mind?"

She nodded.

"Like me and Troll?"

"No. Not the Troll so much. More like you and Gosling." She must have caught the perplexed look on my face because she continued. "It's kind of like a radio signal. Some are stronger than others. Or think of it like eavesdropping on a conversation. Or another way to think of it is like a memory, a glimpse of something, but it's not my memory, it's about what will happen. Does that make sense?"

I nodded, although really it didn't make sense. How could it? I pictured a movie running at the edge of her mind. It was spinning too fast to watch, but every so often it would slow down just enough so she could get a peek.

"Interesting," I said, skeptically. "So you just catch a piece of something?"

"Normally yeah, that's it. That's how I knew you were going to see Gosling. I picked up a signal as you were stepping into that funky car."

I nodded. Car tires screeched outside.

"I see," I said. "So do you make a habit of letting people know you have access to their thoughts?"

"Early on, yeah, I did, but now mostly no. Really, almost never – it's been years." She tilted her head to one side. "Most people don't respond well."

"Why make an exception with me?"

"Don't be stupid."

An image of her bent over the side of the bed danced across my mind, and I wondered – since she was a mind reader – if she saw it. "Maybe you should go to Vegas and wait for a glimpse of whether the roulette ball will land on black or red."

"It only works with people, not inanimate objects. And besides, I can't direct it toward what I want."

"Never?"

"No. I can't predict where a parking spot will open up, or which sports team will win. It's not really useful, in a practical sense. If someone asked, I couldn't predict their future."

"So how do you explain this special power?"

"I can't. Although my suspicion is that it has something to do with my ear, or my lack of an ear." She used her hand to press her hair against her head, protectively, like she'd done at the Italian restaurant the night before. "Maybe when nature takes something away it compensates in other ways? At least that's my theory."

We sat in an eerie stillness for a good while. I tried to process what she had told me, but my mind – which was still feeling decidedly hazy from the weed I'd smoked – refused to work at full capacity.

I eventually broke the silence. "So you said you normally just get a small glimpse of something, but not always?"

She nodded.

"Sometimes you see something more?"

Another nod.

I took a stab in the dark, an educated guess. "And you've seen something more with the Troll?"

She paused, bit her lip, and then answered, "Yes."

"Such as..."

She let out a long sigh, blinked, and when her eyelids opened her pupils appeared to take on a different, more yellowish hue.

"When I was thirteen," she began, "my unconscious began to start working in overtime. As I've told you, I'd gotten flashed insights before – I knew I was a little different than most people – but these visions came to me exclusively during the daytime. Now at thirteen, my dreams, which had been so banal in the past, twisted into something more profound. At least that's how I interpreted them. They were vivid and as colorful and coherent as a feature film. These dreams returned to me nightly for a solid year, maybe a little longer. They were pleasant, something that I looked forward to. Each night when I laid my head down on the pillow I knew what was coming."

Nika cleared her throat. I felt the fogginess in my mind clear up just a bit. I rested my head on the pillow and let her voice wash over me.

"The dreams were never exactly the same," she continued, "but they didn't vary much. There was an apartment building in a seedy section of a city. The paint was chipped, the front lawn completely uncared for, men holding bottles stuffed inside brown paper bags loitered near the front steps. It was squalid. I'd start with a bird's eye view of the building, maybe one hundred feet up, and then pan in. I'd slowly zoom toward one of the building's windows – always on the third floor – until I moved inside the room."

Nika pulled her legs tightly to her chest, wrapped her arms around her knees.

"The room inside was nice enough," she continued, "nicer than the outside of the building, although it definitely was not elegant. It was functional, but cluttered. There were books everywhere. And notepads filled with writing and computers of all shapes and sizes and electronics components scattered around. In the middle of all of it was the Troll."

She squeezed her knees tighter.

"I couldn't take my eyes off him. He was magnetic.

You hear stories about people who have so much charisma they literally change the feeling of a room when they enter it. That was the Troll. He just had that *it* quality. His charisma shone through despite the fact that he wasn't really doing anything, at least not what people would normally finding compelling to watch. He'd tinker with one of the electronic devices or jot down notes on a sheet of paper or work on the computers. Mostly he sat quietly and thought."

"Just sat there and thought?" I asked.

"That right. He had a large wingchair where he'd sit quietly for hours and just think. I never knew what he was thinking about, but for some reason watching him was spellbinding. I could tell he was concentrating deeply, trying to solve a difficult riddle or make some type of breakthrough. All his thinking and tinkering only happened at night. He'd start latish, let's say around ten, and then keep at it until three or four in the morning. And as far as I could tell, he'd sleep most of the day, although I can't really be sure because I never saw him during the daytime, only at night."

When Nika reached this point in the story the yellow in her eyes seemed to fade away and she became noticeably tired. I didn't say anything, hoping she would tell me more, but instead she slumped down into the bed, rested her head on the pillow, and cinched the covers up tight under her chin.

"So is that all?" I asked, eventually.

"Essentially. I had these dreams over and over for a year, so I could go into a lot more detail. But the rest is more of the same. And then one day, when I was fourteen, the dreams just stopped."

I pulled myself up a little in the bed, rested my back on the headboard. "So you haven't dreamed about any of this since then?"

"Not until the other night, the night I saw you with the Troll."

Her eyes dropped shut and I was afraid she'd fallen asleep. I gently shook her shoulder. "You dreamt about me and the Troll?"

"That's right," she said. And with her eyes closed she recounted my entire visit with the Troll, not leaving out a single detail. Any doubts that I may have still held regarding her psychic abilities were gone. She'd clearly seen what I had seen. But it had also clarified another point for me: the reason Nika had asked me to dinner that day in the coffee room was because she wanted to learn more about the Troll.

She wasn't really interested in me. But then I thought about Whitfield's advice; maybe it wasn't all bad? Or at least I'd worry about it another day.

As these thoughts worked through my mind Nika rolled onto her side, cracked open her eyes, and with her head still resting on her pillow said in a husky whisper, "So, you still haven't told me what Gosling said."

I shrugged. "Not much." I lied. I'm not sure why, but I did. "He'd heard of the Troll, but only had secondhand knowledge. We mostly talked about Centre Terrain."

From the look on Nika's face I gathered that she wasn't buying it. "But he confirmed that the Troll really does exist?"

I nodded.

"So what did he look like?" she asked.

"Gosling?"

"Uh-huh."

I told her. Then something occurred to me. "Have you noticed that in books and movies it's often older men, like Gosling, who provide important pieces of backstory?" I asked.

"No, I hadn't."

"Well take the *Maltese Falcon*. It's the Fat Man who tells

Spade about the history of the black bird." Nika looked puzzled. I continued. "A jewel encrusted statue given to the king of Spain by the Knight Templars of Malta? Stolen by pirates?" Her face was a complete blank. "So you've never read the book, seen the movie?"

"No and no."

She yawned. I yawned. She rubbed her eyes.

Although it was clear that sleep was coming, I decided to give her a little trivia. "I read that the Maltese Falcon – the statue used in the movie – is actually the most prized artifact of all movie collectables. It's the title of the book, the title of the movie, and the plot revolves around it."

Without missing a beat she responded, "What about the ring in those hobbit books?"

She had a point.

"Anyway, another old man is Lebowski in *The Big Lebowski*. Not the Dude, but the villain in the wheelchair."

"Sorry." She yawned again.

"No. You can't be serious. You've never seen *The Big Lebowski*?"

She shook her head, her eyes shut.

"That's criminal. You've been deprived. It's possible that I've seen that movie fifty times."

"You're kidding."

"No, I'm not. I have it memorized. Those characters are as real to me as my friends, more so."

"You really are a bit compulsive."

I ignored that comment. "We'll watch it together."

"Part of our loafing routine?"

"Exactly." It was my turn to yawn.

"Now let's hit the sack," she said. She flipped over so her back faced me. She took my arm, tugged me close to her. "Spoon me," she said, and we drifted off to sleep.

26

'd been back in the Bay Area for just a week when I was contacted by a recruiter for Centre Terrain. By then I'd started to give up hope of finding the Captain. At the time I was living in a motel room on Columbus Ave., a place that scraped against the outer fringe of Fisherman's Wharf. I was toying with the idea of returning to Italy when I got the call.

"Are you interested in a job?" she, the recruiter, asked me over the phone.

"What type of job?"

"You'd be a programmer."

"What type of programmer?"

She provided a rough sketch of what Centre Terrain was all about. It sounded odd, a little interesting, but not something I was eager to do. She must have sensed my hesitancy, because she said, "It pays very well."

"How well?"

She threw out a figure. I was impressed.

"And there's a signing bonus."

"There is..."

"Yes, it's one hundred thousand dollars."

That, obviously, was a sizeable bonus. I'd heard of bigger: Microsoft and Google had once fought over a talented programmer, each offering a signing bonus of a million dollars. But still, this was large.

"Why don't you come over to our office and we can discuss it," the recruiter said.

At the Centre Terrain headquarters I was shown a

demo of the game. They gave me a pair of augmentation glasses and I went on a test drive. It was cool. I hadn't been aware that the game existed, but I could feel myself getting hooked, even with just one go at it.

Then we talked about the bonus.

"There's something you need to do to earn it," I was told.

That something was getting the processor installed. Naturally, I didn't like the idea. Who would? But I was assured the procedure would be quick and painless and that once I had the processor I would like the result.

"If you think you're a good programmer now," the recruiter told me, "just wait. You'll see."

They set up meetings with three current Sweepers, all of whom touted the benefits of the device.

"Dude, you'll like it," one of them told me. "It's like, I don't know, cool. You can code a lot faster."

I heard similar – if slightly more eloquent – stories from the others. All of them convinced me that the operation was nothing to worry about.

And it wasn't.

"Just close your eyes and relax," a doctor told me as I was stretched out on an operating table.

A few hours later I was awake and in my hospital room. I felt fine. I was told that there was a miniscule scar on the back of my head, but I couldn't see it, and noticed no other differences. I felt good enough to go home, but as a precaution I had to stay overnight.

Hospitals at night are sad and creepy places. All the employees are dressed in the same drab uniforms. The patients are sick. There is a lingering aroma of death and illness. That night I had trouble sleeping so I took a stroll on the floor, ending up in the dreary little TV room. Nika was there, although I didn't know who she was at the time. Her hair was the same lollipop red, but no raccoon eyes.

She didn't look at me when I walked in the door. She just kept her eyes glued to the TV screen, which was showing a rerun of *The Big Bang Theory*. I sat down on a plastic chair and watched the show, all the while sneaking peeks at Nika through the corner of my eye.

"I suppose I should be a fan of this program," I said, "but I've never really been able to get into it."

"The TV is broken. You can't change the channel. This is the only option," she informed me, without taking her eyes off the screen.

That was it – we didn't exchange another word that night.

Not the next day, either. And this despite the fact that Nika and I checked out of the hospital at the same time; she stood right next to me, both of us filling out forms, but she treated me like I didn't exist. At the time, I didn't know she was going to be a fellow Sweeper. I learned that my first day on the job – she was there, in the orientation room, when I arrived. She didn't so much as say "hi." Besides the comment about the TV being broken, I can't recall her saying two words to me, not until that day in the coffee room when she asked me out to dinner.

But putting that aside, the neural processor had bolstered my ability to write code. The improvement was apparent immediately. If anything, the recruiter had downplayed the enhancement. I was Barry Bonds on steroids, or, really, Roma was because what I could do in Centre Terrain couldn't be duplicated outside. It would be impossible for my real-life fingers to keep pace with my processor-enhanced brain. But inside I was a beast.

27

The next morning Nika and I took the 71 Haight-Noriega to work. It reeked of fresh vomit. Along for the ride were other commuters and a handful of grungy, drugged-up teenagers. It was a long trip because the bus snaked through a number of neighborhoods before finally depositing us in the Financial District. Throughout the ride we never once discussed the Troll or the story that Nika had told me the night before.

We'd decided to go into the Centre Terrain building separately, not wanting people to know about our budding relationship. Nika went first, and I waited outside a few minutes before riding up the elevator. Once on the fifth floor, I got a cup of coffee and started toward the Sweeper room, but as soon as I exited the coffee area Edzard appeared and blocked my path.

"We need to talk," he said.

A minute later we were seated in his office. The papers on his desk were stacked even higher. "We're putting you on probation," he said. His face looked twisted, like he was holding in a shit.

"What? Why?"

"That stunt you pulled yesterday. It was in violation of a key company rule. It has caused a boatload of problems."

"Like what?"

"I'm not going to get into it with you."

"But I thought the CEO liked my video?"

"His view has changed."

Classic and predictable: from what I'd witnessed his views changed constantly, often depending on whom he'd spoken with last, and he invariably landed on the wrong decision. It was a miracle that Centre Terrain was so damn profitable.

"Listen," Edzard continued, "you and I both know this is overdue. Okay? Yesterday was just the final straw. You're a great programmer, and the company has a lot invested in you. But there is more to the job than just sweeping."

I looked up at the ceiling, let the news sink in. One of the florescent lights was flickering.

"So what exactly does being on probation mean?" I asked.

"It means you don't come to work. It means you won't get paid."

"For how long?"

"Indefinite. But you're still an employee, so you'll still get benefits. And if deemed appropriate, there's always the chance that we'll end the probation at some point in the future."

During my time at Polpo, I'd witnessed the unpleasant task of employee layoffs, so I knew that an individual was powerless to stop it. I also didn't want to give Edzard the satisfaction of seeing me commit an emotional outburst, so I said nothing, accepted my fate stoically.

"I'm going to leave now," he said. "You need to sign some paperwork. Someone from HR will be here in a minute."

He left without even saying good luck.

28

The Captain had handled all of the arrangements associated with the dissolving of Polpo. He was the one who contacted Google and got the acquisition ball rolling. He, along with some lawyers, negotiated the final payout. He met with the investors to assure them that they would be paid off first. He did more – much more, I'm sure – but I wasn't aware of all the details. Ostensibly that was because the Captain and I decided it was better if I focused on programming, improving the Polpo product so that when the company was ultimately sold it would generate a bigger payout. But in reality I didn't want to know. I tried to block out the fact that Polpo was dying.

≈≈≈

On the last day of the company's existence I was in the Captain's office. It was ten a.m. and he'd scheduled a company All Hands meeting for eleven. Together we were going to let everyone know that Polpo was shutting its doors. An air of unease and anticipation floated throughout the building. It was so palpable it felt like you could reach out and touch it. The employees knew something was up, something bad, it just wasn't clear yet to them how bad.

The Captain opened the top drawer of his desk. He pulled out a check, handed it me. "Don't spend it all in one place," he said.

I read the amount. It was a lot, seven figures. "Where'd you get this?" I asked.

He looked at me like I was crazy. "What do you mean,

where did I get this? We sold our assets. We didn't make enough to even come close to paying off the other investors, but they got some. That's your severance."

"This is a generous amount of money," I said. "Enough to last for, I don't know, a while."

The Captain said, "You earned it."

"And what about the employees?"

There weren't a lot of employees, just a few hundred, but they were a dedicated bunch. They worked long hours, weekends, in most cases took less in salary than if they'd worked at one of the established companies in the Valley. Of course, that's part of the arrangement when you latch on with a start-up; you're rolling the dice that some short-term pain will result in a big payoff. Sometimes it does, more often it doesn't.

The Captain just shook his head.

"Nothing?" I asked.

"Not even two weeks." He shrugged, as if it were completely out of his hands. "They knew the deal."

I was hit with a wave of guilt. I'd just been handed a large check. It was big enough that if I'd spread it around it would have softened the blow for some of our employees, not all, but some, definitely more than just me.

But I didn't spread it around. I kept the money for myself.

≈≈≈

The next day I woke up to the realization that I had nothing to do. There were no staff meetings or customer calls, no updating the product roadmap or fixing bugs, no interviewing potential new employees or consulting with finance. Nothing. Really, there was no reason for me to get out of bed.

So I didn't.

I stayed tucked under the sheets the next day as well, and the day after that, and the day after that, and then one more day. I didn't eat a bite, but each night I drank at least three Bloody Marys. I didn't shower. My dreams were filled with bizarre, frightening nightmares.

When I woke on the morning of the fifth day I noticed a fly in my room. I watched as be buzzed from wall to wall. In time, I noticed a coherent flight pattern, a symmetrical loop orchestrated with impressive precision. The fly was executing a series of aerial acrobatics that would make the Blue Angels proud. It was a sight to see; my eyes stayed transfixed, amazed. After a perfect loop-de-loop, the fly stopped in mid-air, hovered a few feet above my head.

It spoke.

"You're a mess," it said.

"Excuse me?"

"You stink. You look emaciated. What's going on?"

What's going on, indeed? I sniffed under an armpit. The fly was right, I reeked. With what seemed like a Herculean effort, I dragged myself out of bed and into the shower. After I'd cleaned up, I ate a piece of toast, half a banana, and drank a large glass of orange juice.

A talking fly – was I losing my mind?

It happens. A person experiences a traumatic event – the death of a loved one, the disappearance of a best friend, the trauma of war – and they snap. The next thing you know they're moved to a white, padded room.

But no one had died. I hadn't lost a friend. What, exactly, had happened to me? I'll tell you what – a company had failed. My company had failed. Big f-ing deal, it happens every day. And people move on. I could move on.

Or could I?

I logged onto my laptop. I had decided it was time to get back to work. I needed to brew up something new. Create a new program. Work toward launching a new company. Get back to my old self. But nothing came out. I had no ideas. I sat at the computer, positioned my hands at the keyboard, but my fingers were unable to move.

At first I wasn't too worried. I chalked it up to just being a little rusty. I'd give it a go the next day and all would be fine. Or so I believed.

It wasn't fine the next day. The same lack of production occurred. And it kept happening, day after day. I'd plop down at my desk, fire up my computer, try to program, but no lines of code would materialize. I was like a novelist hit with a fierce case of writer's block.

But I didn't give in, at least not at first. Each morning I'd stumble out of bed, shower, eat a light breakfast, sit down at my desk, and get to work. I kept a log of how much time I spent at the computer, promised myself that I'd sit there for at least two hours. And I did, every day for two weeks. Nada. Not a line of code was produced.

The fly reappeared. He danced through the air and then landed on top of my laptop.

"You need a change of scenery," he said.

The fly was right.

I logged onto a travel site and bought a first-class ticket and flew to Italy.

Part Two

29

The meeting with the Centre Terrain human resources manager took less than a half hour and then I was back outside, on the sidewalk. I felt like a balloon drained of helium, depleted, collapsing to the sidewalk, but then, just like that, the expansive feelings of happiness and goodwill started to well inside me, first slowly and then quickly, like the victim of a car accident who realizes the other guy's insurance will buy him a brand new car. The sun picked that very moment to burst through a tear in the clouds. A pretty woman smiled as she hurriedly brushed past me. A bus horn wailed. The chaotic sounds of children at play arrived from somewhere nearby.

I didn't have to work! I was free! True, without my salary I'd have to dig into my Polpo savings, but that was okay, I had money to spare. Besides, there was a lot I wanted to think about, mainly the Troll, and the stories I'd heard from Gosling and Nika. And now I had free time to ponder their meaning.

I started to walk down the sidewalk.

I only made it a block before a long black limousine slid alongside me and pulled to a stop at the curb. The car's backdoor opened and from inside a deep voice ordered, "Get in." Before I could make a move, the front passenger door opened and out stepped a man built like an exceptionally large refrigerator. He was rectangular and thick, he wore a black suit and black tie, since he had no neck his head rested directly on his shoulders. He didn't say a word, but grabbed me by my forearm, tossed me into the backseat like a toy, then shut the door. He climbed back into the passenger seat and we sped away.

The air inside the limo was heavy with B.O. The stench was almost debilitating, so strong it made my eyes burn.

"Can we crack a window?" I asked, and wiped away some tears.

No response.

The car kept moving. I took an audit of my surroundings. There were three men in the car with me: driver, front passenger seat, and a man pressed into the backseat next to me. All three wore the same black suit and black tie uniform. I became gripped with the fearful realization that my life was about to end. I was going to be killed, cement shoes attached to my feet, and tossed into the bay.

But why?

"You guys are taking a real risk, not wearing your seatbelts," I said, trying to joke past my fear. I latched myself in with my own seatbelt, but the thugs didn't make a move to follow my lead.

It didn't matter. Three turns of the limo and the driver steered us into an underground garage. He eased that mammoth car into a slotted parking spot. The giant in the front passenger seat opened his door, stepped out, and pulled my door open.

"Move," he snarled.

The air in the parking garage was stifling, but eons better than the limo. Together the four of us walked from the car to an elevator. I imagined we resembled one of those learning puzzles designed for young school children: circle the man that doesn't look like he belongs with the other two.

When the elevator doors opened the four of us crammed inside, although it was a tight squeeze. As soon as the doors slid shut the space filled with the wretched stench of B.O. I stood directly under one of the giants' armpits. The odor was so powerful I started to gag. And unfortunately, it didn't look like it would be a short ride, because the beast who'd thrown me into the backseat of the limo hit the button for the top floor.

"So what's going on?" I managed to force out between gasps for breath, as we ascended. "Where are we going?"

No response – crickets.

One of the thugs must have farted, because the smell got even worse, if you can believe it. It was a putrid mix of B.O. and rotten eggs. I wanted to puke. I might have fainted, but it was so crammed inside that elevator that it would have been impossible to fall down.

After what felt like a lifetime the elevator reached its destination. The doors opened, I was pushed out. The giants, thankfully, stayed inside and soon were gone.

In stark contrast to the elevator, the room I'd entered smelled good, like fresh flowers, and I took note that there were, in fact, vases scattered about with what appeared to newly cut arrangements. The problem was that I could just barely appreciate the smell. The B.O. had been so strong it still lingered in my nostrils.

It was an odd room with high ceilings and shiny white walls. There were four skylights and four large windows, but the windows were so high up I couldn't see out them. There was a hardwood floor and a white rug and a glass-top coffee table that was surrounded by a couple of love seats. There were also a few aqua-colored armchairs.

The morning had been particularly hectic – being put on probation, kidnapped – and I took a moment to catch my breath. But a moment was all I had, because a man stepped through a side door and walked toward me. He was clean-cut and I pegged him as mid-thirties. He wore a natty white suit and bright red shirt, untucked.

"Hi, I'm Roderick Jaynes. Can I get you some water?

We have flat or sparkling."

When he spoke I felt a shadow, a wintry presence escape into the air. It made me edgy. His voice was odd. I thought I detected a hint of an English accent. Or maybe it was Minnesotan, so latent it was almost non-existent.

"What I could use is an oxygen mask," I answered.

He smiled, toothlessly. "My compatriots do have a smell about them, don't they? Perhaps I should suggest they take a periodic bath."

"More like a full-body salt scrub down."

Who was this douche?

"I'm gathering you'd like to get down to cases," Jaynes said. He delivered it just like a line out of a movie. The guy was a piece of work, a real tool, I could tell that much already.

"Come with me then," Jaynes beckoned. He led me to the middle of the room. Jaynes sat in one of the aqua chairs, and I plopped down on a loveseat. "So tell me what progress you've made finding the Troll."

The Troll, that's what this was about.

"Excuse me..." I said.

"The Troll, have you found him?"

"I don't know what you're talking about."

Jaynes smiled again. "Come now, don't be coy, we both know you're lying. So tell me, what have you learned?"

I paused a bit before saying, "Nothing to report – bits and pieces is all." Who was this asshole, anyway?

"He visited you one time, is that right?"

"How'd you know that? Do you work for the NSA or something?"

This elicited a smirk. "The government, that's laughable. No, definitely not. I'm a special assistant to a venture capitalist, a very important man. The man I represent is keenly interested in learning more about the

Troll."

Another fucking VC, I should have seen that coming. Although I'd classify Jaynes – and the man he ostensibly represented – as more of a vulture capitalist.

"I see," I said, and tried to lend an air of disapproval to my remark.

"Surely Gosling told you there would be other interested parties?"

Me: "It must have slipped his mind."

Jaynes: "So what *did* Gosling tell you about the Troll?"

As if I was going to tell him anything. "Nothing significant," I lied. "Mainly stories about high school basketball."

This didn't sit too well with him. He leaned toward me. "You make jokes, but have you given any thought to the potential of what the Troll can offer?"

In truth, I had, a little. Although it wasn't really clear to me what the Troll was proposing, if anything. I'd seen him float around a room, give me some cryptic clues, but there was nothing concrete. Hell, I wasn't even really clear that he was offering me something. But clearly Jaynes saw some potential.

"So that's why you dragged my here?" I asked. "So you can make more money?" It was a little belated, but I could finally feel my blood boil. "Kidnapping is a federal offense."

"Make more money, you say." He gave me a wicked grin. "Do you have any concept of the amount of money we're talking about here?"

I shrugged.

"It's not sports star money," he scoffed. "No. That's thinking far too small. I'm talking about *real* wealth, Bill Gates-level. Okay. The type of money required to mold history. You've been an entrepreneur. Surely you can appreciate the start-up opportunity. And since you have the connection with the Troll, you're in a position to call the shots. CEO, CTO – whatever sails your boat."

"And you're the money man."

"That's right. Or my associate is. And this could be just the start. It gives us a chance to expand into a new line of business."

"What line of business are you in now?"

He squirmed a little. "We have a finger in a lot of different projects. Core hardware and software, sure. But really we're focused on cross-platform integration and new generations of distributed computing. Global networks, multi-client. Next gen business and consumer applications, all cloud-based and easily downloadable. Smart computing. And we dabble somewhat into social networking. Everything cutting edge. Recognizing paradigm shifts, and the ability to see around corners – those are really keys. We identify market transitions and work to get out ahead of them. "

Paradigm shifts, market transitions? To stifle a laugh, I bit my lower lip so hard I nearly broke the skin. This guy talked in marketing gibberish.

Jaynes stood. He walked toward the back of the room, away from the windows, to a kitchenette. Over his shoulder he said, "So I take it you don't really have any news from the Troll?"

Not anything that I wanted to share. "Not at this point," I said. "But if we put together some type of arrangement, I can keep you informed." Hell, with the probation, I would need a new source of income. Maybe I could milk this dickwad?

He returned to where I sat. He held a small plate. On the plate were two brownies. "Arrangement – that could work. I'll have someone put together the paperwork. To seal the deal, join me in a little snack." He extended the plate toward me.

"No thanks. I normally avoid desserts."

"Nonsense. I love to bake and take particular pride in my brownies. So I insist."

He baked? Right...

So once again someone insisted that I partake in his vice of choice. First it was a mojito, next a brownie. But this time it was different, I knew that much. I'd seen enough B movies to understand that Jaynes' offer smelled fishy. Better yet, I smelled a skunk, but I knew I needed to hold my nose and eat the brownie anyway. Really, what option did I have? I could decline again, force Jaynes' hand, but I assumed the card he'd play would be to call his hulkish, putrid thugs into the room and have them force the dessert down my throat. No, I didn't want that. It seemed easier to just eat a fucking brownie and wait for the consequences.

"All right, if you twist my arm," I said.

I plucked a square off the plate, took a bite. It was damn good. Actually, better than simply good, it was mouthwatering. I took another bite, before pushing the entire thing into my mouth. "You know your way around the kitchen, Jaynes," I said as I licked the crumbs off my fingertips. "Do I detect a little bit of fudge in here?"

Suddenly my head felt swollen. My eyesight blurred. Rubbing my forehead I said, "I don't think I've fully recovered from that B.O." I looked at Jaynes. He faded in and out of focus. Next there were two of him, then three. The last thing I remember saying was, "I need to lie down..."

30

Darkness.

It was as dark as the time I was visited by the Troll, charcoal black, not a pinprick of light. Only this darkness had a different quality than before: not welcoming, but ominous.

Far in the distance a figure appeared. It was the shape of a person and it moved toward me, floated through space. Behind this person was a bright, white light. I could make out no specific features, other than the silhouetted shape of a human body. The light grew brighter as the figure neared me. At first I assumed that the black frame was the Troll, but as it slid forward it became clear the person was too short. Then I saw that it was a woman. Then I could make out her face: Nika. She was decked out all in black, thigh-high boots and a miniskirt. She wore a bustier that squeezed her breasts together and upward. I fought the urge to reach out and grab them. On Nika's head, just a little off center, was a tall, black crown. She looked regal and impossibly seductive.

The song "Trojans" by *Atlas Genius* – the song I'd been fixated on – started to play all around me, as if it was being piped in by unseen speakers. "There's Trojans in my head..."

Nika approached me. She put a forefinger under my chin, lifted me upward, and spun me in a circle so that my body was parallel to the ground.

After a few rotations I broke free, somersaulted,

crashed to the ground.

I got to my feet, started to run, but although my legs spun rapidly I made no progress, like a cartoon character. I was locked in place, tethered by an invisible string. Below me an enormous black-and-white chessboard appeared. The song in the air changed; it was still the same tune, but morphed into a bastardized Muzak version.

Looking over my shoulder, I saw Nika standing, posed like a soldier, her legs spread in a V, hands on hips. Behind her an army of black-and-white chess pieces appeared. Nika looked right, left, back toward me. She pointed, her arm stretched to its full extent. Her army started to pursue me, or at least tried to, because they too just ran in place.

But then a black rook broke from the pack, hurtled toward me, and just before it reached my head it morphed into Jaynes. I ducked and he flew past.

Next the white queen flew in. Seconds before hitting me it turned into Priya. I avoided it but not completely; she brushed my left shoulder.

In front of me, a giant arm appeared from above, nothing else, just an arm, the portion from the hand to mid-bicep. It resembled the arm of God reaching down from the heavens; only it wasn't God's arm, but the Troll's. How did I know that? I can't explain it, I just did. I kept running and as I ran a metal hamster wheel formed around me. It spun and spun and spun and I frantically raced to keep up. Pinched between the Troll's thumb and forefinger was a tall chess piece, the black king. The Troll planted the king directly in front of me, just beyond the reach of the wire grates of the spinning wheel, and his arm disappeared. I kept running and running and running. Strands of blue binary code appeared all around me, zeroes and ones zoomed here and there and back again. These vanished and were replaced by 3-D spheres with Y and X axes. I ran and ran and ran, but no matter how fast I went I could never reach the black king.

≈ ≈ ≈

The Muzak stopped, the hallucination ended.

I was stretched out on cold, merciless pavement. I felt clawing at my feet. My left shoe had been removed, and it seemed someone was in the process of trying to take the right one. I pulled my leg back, knee to chest, opened my eyes, and took in the sight of a homeless man. He greedily clutched my stolen shoe to his breast. In his hand he squeezed an iPhone, which, by the beleaguered look of him, I assumed he couldn't afford, and deduced that he'd burglarized it from me as well.

"H ... h ... hey ..." I said, although I had trouble getting the word out.

"Mine!" the homeless man declared, his face scrunched in a ferocious scowl. "Mine, mine!" He turned, shuffled down the sidewalk, disappeared into an alley.

I was in no mood to pursue. My head ached. It felt like it might split in two. It took a few moments to gather my bearings. In time, I recognized that I was lying prone in a storefront doorway in the middle of Chinatown, on Grant Street. People walked past me – tourists, shop vendors – but not one of them paid me any attention, no one offered to help me off the ground. So I pushed myself up. My head cleared, if only slightly, and I detected the unmistakable smell of urine. My pant leg was wet and I wondered if I'd peed myself. It was nearly dark, dusk. How long had I been out? Scanning the area, I saw red and yellow banners strung across the street and attached on either end to a building. I stood motionless for a few minutes, allowed myself to adjust to my surroundings. Eventually, I hobbled down the street, step by step, slowly, painfully, the pavement biting my exposed foot, up one hill, up a steeper one, encased in fog, up the staircase inside my apartment building, up three floors, until I made it to the door of my unit, opened it, took one step, another, a third, and into my bedroom. I collapsed onto my mattress. Magnus Carlsen was fast asleep at the foot of the bed. I passed out before my head touched the pillow.

31

My intercom rang, rattled my bedroom. There were two short rings, and then a long extended one, like someone was leaning on the downstairs buzzer. I fell out of bed and rushed to answer it, hoping it was Nika. It wasn't, it was Priya, and she asked if she could come up and see me. "Sure," I said, and hit the button that unlocked the door to the building.

"What happened to you?" she asked, once inside my apartment. I'd moved over to the sofa. "I'm sorry, but you look *awful*. It looks like you slept in your clothes. And you're still wearing one shoe."

"It's been a rough twenty-four hours."

"I tried to call you on your cell phone, but there was something wrong with the connection."

"Someone stole it. And he stole one of my shoes." Using the ball of my foot, I pushed off the shoe that remained on my foot, the shoe I'd slept in. "My head is killing me," I complained, and rubbed a hand through my hair. There was an intense throbbing sensation behind my right eye – boom, boom.

Magnus Carlsen took that moment to jump out of bed and he started meowing loudly for his breakfast.

"Go take an Advil and a shower. I'll feed your cat," Priya offered. She looked at Magnus and asked, "What's his name?"

"Magnus Carlsen."

"*Magnus Carlsen* – that's an odd name for a cat."

I was too wiped to even muster a shrug.

"Have you eaten yet?" she asked.

"No." I felt a sharp stab of hungry and my stomach growled in protest over my neglect of it.

Priya's eyes opened a little wider, as if she'd heard the growl. "Do you have food in the fridge?"

"Yeah, maybe, I'm not sure. They're probably some eggs, toast, possibly something else. It's been awhile since I've shopped."

"I'll rummage. Do you drink coffee?"

"The stronger the better."

Magnus jumped up on the sofa, rubbed his head against my arm, meowed louder.

"You go get cleaned up," Priya said, "I'll make some breakfast and feed Magnus Carlsen."

"There's tuna for him in one of the cabinets. And milk in the refrigerator." I walked toward the bathroom. Just before arriving at the door I asked, "What time is it anyway?"

"11:30," Priya hollered from inside the kitchen.

≈≈≈

It was a long shower. Epic. Before climbing in, I did take two Advil. I let the hot water beat down on my head for much longer than normal. My headache started to fade away, marginally, just enough to make me feel human again. Using body wash, I scrubbed every inch of myself, let the water rinse off the soap, and then coated myself again. I wanted to fully remove the stench of the street.

Afterward, I shaved, brushed my teeth, flossed, brushed my teeth again, and rinsed my mouth with mouthwash. I even used some clippers to trim my nose hairs. I donned my robe, which I'd left hanging on the bathroom door hook, walked to my bedroom, and put on a fresh pair of jeans, a black T-shirt, and a pair of socks. Magnus Carlsen had already returned to the foot of the bed, where he was giving himself a thorough tongue

166

cleaning. He looked contented.

I smelled coffee. My stomach rumbled again.

"I'm in here," Priya's voice floated in from the living room.

As I walked through the French doors I took in the sight of Priya seated at the little table inside my bay window. There was sunshine. "Sit down, eat," she ordered.

I followed her command. Spread on a plate before me was an enormous ham and cheese omelet, grilled potatoes and a toasted bagel with cream cheese. There was also a bowl with chunks of cantaloupe. My mug was filled and the coffee steamed, and she'd even poured a large cup of orange juice.

"I wasn't sure how you took your coffee, so I brought both half-and-half and sugar."

Miss Efficient strikes again.

"This is amazing," I said, and I dug in with gusto. "Really – *amazing*. Thank you, thank you, thank you."

"Your kitchen is surprisingly functional, for a man."

I ignored the reverse sexism of her comment.

"Your copper pans are great. Do you cook?"

"Sure," I said, between bites. "Lots of pasta. But also soups and stews and chili and other comfort foods." I noticed that she wasn't eating. "Aren't you hungry?"

"I had breakfast long ago. And I nibbled while preparing yours, so I'm okay for a while longer. This coffee should do me." She lifted her cup to her lips.

For the next few minutes we didn't talk. She drank and I ate.

The omelet was scrumptious and the potatoes grilled to perfection; the cream cheese-covered bagel hit the spot. I devoured it all like a man released from prison, and then went to work on the cantaloupe.

"You're an angel," I said, finally finished, and I leaned back in my chair. I had to stifle a burp. My headache had miraculously vanished.

"Thank you." She seemed pleased, a woman happy with a job well done. "So you said someone stole your cell phone?"

My phone, that's right, it was gone. I had pushed the incident with the homeless man out of my mind, at least momentarily, while I ate, along with everything that had happened the previous day. Maybe sometimes, when in need of repose, the human brain can block out unpleasant thoughts? But stubborn facts remained: I was effectively out of a job, I had been kidnapped and drugged, and I had no cell phone. I wondered if Nika had tried to contact me.

And I wasn't any closer to finding the Troll.

"That's right," I said. "My phone was stolen."

"So what happened?"

I didn't feel like reliving the entire episode, so I just said, "It's a long story. Is it okay if I fill you in later?"

"Fair enough. But since you don't have a phone, maybe now would be a good time for you to help me get an iPhone? What do you think?"

"Yeah, sure, why not?" It wasn't as if I had anything else planned. "Should we go now?"

"Let's go." As we stood she said, in an offhand way, "Oh, I also have an offer from Mr. Gosling that I'd like to discuss."

"Oh yeah, what is it?"

"I'll fill you in later," she said.

≈≈≈

Priya had driven up from the Peninsula and parked her car in a garage near my apartment, but we didn't feel like retrieving it and fighting through city traffic, so instead we walked to the Fairmount Hotel and hopped into a cab, and in no time we arrived at the Apple store on Market Street. Predictably, the place was packed with shoppers, but one of the red shirted sales clerks –

ostentatiously named a "Genius" – stepped up and helped us with our purchases. In no time we were out the door with two new iPhones, lickety-split.

As we walked down the sidewalk, I turned my phone on, hoping that Nika had called or sent a text. She hadn't. So I sent her a text: *Hi. What's shaking?*

Priya asked if I could give her a tutorial on her new device, so we found a coffee shop, a little hideaway tucked back at the end an alley. Once inside we ordered two large cappuccinos, found a free table, and I walked her through the phone's standard features.

"You can connect to your email. Download songs. Take photographs. And my favorite feature is Maps."

"Maps?"

"It's a GPS tool." That brought a quizzical look to her face, so I elaborated. "Global Positioning System – it uses satellites to identify your location, and it can also give directions to where you want to go. It's pure genius. You'll never get lost again."

"I see," she said. Not that I imagined the ever efficient Priya was prone to getting lost.

"And you can go here to download apps," I said, and with my finger I hit the app button.

"Apps?"

She really was clueless. "Apps is short for applications. There are thousands of them. Games, checkbooks, you can download magazines, podcasts, what have you."

"I see," she said again. She picked the phone up and started caressing it, instinctually, the way people do. "There's a lot to absorb."

"You'll get the hang of it. In no time you'll wonder how you ever lived without one."

She nodded, but without conviction. There was a lull in the conversation as we both sipped our drinks. Priya broke the silence by saying, "So you promised to tell me about your day yesterday."

"I did?"

"Yes, you did." She cocked her head to the side and waited for me to respond.

"All right, here goes..."

I ran through the events of the previous day, start to finish, although I left out the bus ride with Nika and also the bizarre brownie-induced hallucination. Priya listened quietly. When I finished she shook her head and said, "Wow. Well that's quite a lot for one day."

"Tell me about it."

"And you walked all the way home?"

"Uh-huh."

"No wonder you looked so wiped out this morning. Are you going to call the police?"

The police: that honestly hadn't occurred to me. Although it seemed like the logical next step, I heard myself saying, "No. I think I'm just going to try and erase the entire episode from my mind."

She nodded, as if that seemed like the right course to her as well. Then she sat up a little straighter in her chair, pressed her hands to her lap. "I'll come clean. I was aware of part of the story."

"You were?"

"Yes. I knew you'd been put on probation." She examined my face, I supposed to see if I had a reaction.

"Gosling, right?"

"That's right. As the angel investor in Centre Terrain, Mr. Gosling is still kept abreast of certain developments at the company, your probation being one of them. Not that he could have prevented it – he has no day-to-day responsibilities – but he does like to be informed."

How nice for Gosling.

"And that brings me to the offer I mentioned this morning. Do you care to hear it?"

"I'm all ears."

"Mr. Gosling has a home in San Francisco that is currently unoccupied, and he's looking for someone to housesit. Mr. Gosling feels more comfortable knowing there is a person present. And since you are now out of work, you seemed like a good candidate."

House sitter, really? I hesitated before responding, a few seconds slipped by, but then I said, "Is it a paying gig?"

"Of course it pays. Mr. Gosling will match your salary from Centre Terrain. And on top of that, he's willing to pay the rent on your apartment, so you'd come out way ahead."

"And all I need to do is look after the house?"

"That's all. There are no real responsibilities other than just being present at the home. Maids and a gardener come weekly and handle all the necessary maintenance. You'd be free to come and go as you please, as long as you spend every night at the home. Think of it as a paid vacation."

I wasn't quite sure how to take the offer. It's true, I did want a new source of income, even if I didn't really need it at the moment. But house sitter wasn't the career path that I envisioned for myself. Not that Sweeper was either, but that was another story.

"Can I think about it?"

"Yes, yes, of course. Take a day or two and mull it over."

I glanced around the shop at all the people guzzling their coffee. They seemed in a hurry to finish, I guessed so they could rush back to their jobs. My eyes rested on a young woman sitting alone in the corner, her hair pulled back, she wore a smart flannel skirt and black leggings. She must have felt the heat of my stare, because she returned my gaze, her lips pinched tight with anxiety, another wage slave. I could feel her anxiety wafting through the air, and suddenly a paid vacation didn't seem so bad.

Fuck it.

What did I need to think about? Nothing – that's what. It was simple: I wanted money and here was a chance to get paid with practically no responsibilities. Besides, maybe I could use the time off to think about my next gig? Or better yet, to think about the Troll – *We're going to change the world.* And I bet Gosling had a killer pad. I could invite Nika over and we could try and decipher what the Troll was after together, as well as engage in some new location screwing.

I dragged my eyes from the skirted, anxious woman and looked back at Priya. "You know what," I said, "I'm done thinking about it. I'll do it."

"Great." She seemed decidedly pleased. I pictured her crossing off an imaginary item on an imaginary to-do list.

"But there's one condition," I said.

"What is it?"

"Magnus needs to come with me."

She smiled, her lips painted with pink lipstick, and I wondered if she and Magnus Carlsen had had a special moment together earlier that morning when I was in the shower. He can be quite the charmer.

"Your Mr. Carlsen is welcome to join you," she said.

≈≈≈

It took some doing, but eventually we hailed a cab which drove us to the parking garage where Priya's car was stored. She paid the fare.

"I can expense it," she explained, as she tucked her wallet back into her purse.

We said our goodbyes. I took a few steps toward my apartment, but then stopped, turned, and watched Priya as she headed in the other direction, her back to me. At that moment, something about her tugged at me; maybe it was just a desire not to be alone, or maybe something more, I can't say for certain. But without thinking I blurted out, "Hey, Priya." She stopped, turned around completely so that she faced me. "Can I talk you into joining me for dinner?"

This was an unusual move for me. Frankly, it might have been unprecedented. I can't remember a date – or pseudo date – where I'd been the one to initiate it.

That's a sad fact to admit. But my innate lack of initiative when it came to the pursuit of women had been overwhelmed by the fact that I just really, really didn't want to see her go.

"Dinner. That sounds good, it does. But I'm sorry – I really should be going."

"Come on. After this morning's breakfast, I owe you."

She seemed to waver, but didn't make a commitment one way or the other.

"We can go to my apartment. It's my turn to cook. It'll be fun – come on." I used my thumbs to point over my shoulder, urged her to join me. Maybe I wasn't such a coward after all.

She thought about it. "So you'll cook. I suppose I can't turn that down, can I?"

"No, that's right, you can't."

"Okay, you convinced me – let's do it."

≈≈≈

Back inside my apartment, I poured us each a large glass of red wine, and then hunted for something – anything – that I could prepare for dinner, but the cupboards were bare. Whatever food I'd had left Priya had used that morning for breakfast.

"I need to make a quick run to the corner grocery store," I told Priya, who sat on the sofa and gently rubbed the top of Magnus Carlsen's head. "I won't be a minute."

She said that was fine. No hurry.

When I returned, I found that she'd tidied up my

apartment. The dishes that we'd used that morning – which had been left on the table – were cleared.

Catching where my eyesight fell, she said, "I washed the dishes, dried them, and hopefully put them back in their proper spots."

"Thank you. But you didn't have to do all that. You're the guest."

"It was no inconvenience. Besides, it's in my nature."

I had a feeling what she was getting at – her Miss Efficient-ness – but I asked anyway, "Your nature?"

"I'm a little compulsive. And detail oriented. Some might even say I go over the top. When something needs to get done, I just go about doing it. Perhaps you'd noticed?"

I almost blurted out that I had noticed. In fact, I'd even created my own little nickname for her. But I caught myself in time, and instead said, "You? Really? No. You strike me as the carefree."

She sighed. "Now you're bullshitting me." She took a sip of wine, the glass almost empty. "This is actually the one thing that mellows me out, wine. Can I have a refill?"

We walked to the kitchen. I poured her another glass then unloaded the bag that I'd carried back from the store.

Priya took a sip, paused, before taking another. "Here's a weird fact about me – I never buy anything without returning it. Well, never is an exaggeration, but almost never. I always find a flaw – a loose thread, a smudge, something. And it's typically a flaw that others wouldn't even notice. But I can feel it eating away at me. And invariably, the second item I get will have a flaw too, so I'll return that as well."

"And the third?"

"That will have a problem too. But by then I'm so exhausted with the whole process that I just keep it."

"So you're never truly happy with anything that you buy?"

"No, that's the funny part. Ultimately I grow to like what I have – at least most of the time. I just need to go through a tortuous process to get there. It's a little messed up. I'm a freak, right?"

I knew better than to comment, so stayed quiet.

She took another sip, sighed again. "Do you return things?"

I'd never returned anything, not once. "No, I don't."

"That's the way most people are."

"Just be glad you don't live in Malaysia. I read you can't return purchases there."

"That's true. But you can challenge it on your credit card."

I laughed. "You've really got it all figured out. So I'm guessing you'll be back at the Apple store tomorrow, getting a new iPhone."

"No, no, I expect that will be an exception. I bet each one is *perfect*, right out of the box." She reached into her pants pocket, pulled out the phone, and used her thumb to unlock the home screen. She played with the buttons a little before returning the device to her pocket. She'd had the iPhone for less than a day, yet she was already hooked. Those damn things are as addictive as crack.

I topped off her glass and then shooed Priya out of the kitchen, leading her back into the living room, where I teed up Bill Evans' *Autumn Leaves* on my stereo. "You just relax while I cook."

She took another sip and settled into the sofa.

I seasoned a slab of pork tenderloin with an assortment of herbs, and then stuck it into the oven to bake. I sliced two sweet potatoes in half, added cinnamon and butter, wrapped them in Saran Wrap, and heated them in the microwave. I boiled water and steamed some asparagus.

While the meat cooked, I set the table, the same one in

the bay window that we'd used in the morning. Priya tried to get up and help, but I told her to sit back down. I shot her a fierce look to let her know I meant business, and she melted back down into her seat.

In time, the food finished cooking and I spread it out on the table.

At first the meal was eaten without much discussion, but once the potatoes and asparagus were gone and only a few bites of pork tenderloin remained, Priya said, "This is delicious. You really are a cook. This beats being in class."

"You go to school?"

"Uh-huh. I'm getting my MBA at Cal. Business administration. I need to complete just a few more courses. But tonight I'm playing hooky."

Berkeley: she didn't fit the mold. She was more of a button-down Ivy League type, or at least Stanford.

"I picked it because they have a nighttime program," she continued. "I wouldn't want to give up working for Mr. Gosling."

"So you like your job?"

"Love it. I know in a lot of ways I'm just a Girl Friday, but during our two years together I've been exposed to every aspect of his business. It has been extremely educational. I've learned more working for him than I have in getting my MBA – it's not even close."

"So what do you want to do, once you've finished school, that is?"

Priya shrugged. "I'm not sure, but something will come up." Then she looked at her watch. "I want to thank you for your help with the iPhone. And dinner, it was fantastic. But I need to be going."

"You do?"

She nodded.

We both put our hands down on the edge of the table at the same time to help push ourselves out of our chairs, and as we did so our pinkies touched. Once upright, we stood fairly close to each other, close enough that I could hear her breathing. It hit me that I should move in for a kiss, or perhaps more – much more, if I played my cards right, Nika and our budding relationship be damned. Some urges you just can't fight. And it's not like Nika and I had ever said we were exclusive, anyway. Besides, she was just using me to learn about the Troll, right? Why shouldn't I try and juggle a couple of women? As these thoughts bounced in my head it dawned on me that Nika had never returned my text. What was up with that? Anyway, here was Priya – beautiful, sexy in her own efficient way – Priya. We'd spent the entire day together, it was late, we were buzzed on good red wine – physical intimacy seemed like the next logical step.

But maybe I waited too long, or maybe there never really was an opportunity. Either way, Priya took a step back and the spell was broken. She said, "So housesitting – can you move into Mr. Gosling's home tomorrow, or is that too soon?"

Playful Priya was gone, Miss Efficient had returned.

"Tomorrow works."

"Great. I'm assuming you'll need time to pack. How about eleven? I'll come up in a car and drive you and Magnus Carlsen over."

I told her that was perfect. I offered to walk her to her car, but she convinced me that she'd be fine on her own.

≈≈≈

I cleared the table, putting the dirty dishes in the sink to soak overnight. I had a lot to think about, but decided to push it off for another day. As I climbed into bed Magnus Carlsen jumped up to join me. I rolled over to the pillow where Nika had rested her head a couple of nights before. It smelled musty, like sex and apricots. For a moment I wished she was in bed with me, but as I examined my feelings deeper I found that I wasn't downcast. In fact, I felt grounded, like my true self for the first time in as long as I could remember.

32

That night I dreamed about a garage. It was small and wooden with two large doors that opened to either side. The doors were shut. I stood at the start of a long and narrow cement driveway, and the garage was at the far end. We – the garage and I – were in a leafy, suburban neighborhood. I walked along the driveway until I arrived at the garage. I swung open the doors. The Captain was inside. He stood in front of a wooden table. His head was down, his brow creased in concentration.

I walked toward him.

When I reached him I could see that spread out on the table were a number of small electronic devices. I couldn't make out what each one was, but I did recognize a calculator and a thermometer. The Captain was working on a device that was roughly the size of a shoebox. Its color could be described as off-white. The metal front of the device had been removed, and with a screwdriver the Captain was fiddling with the electronics inside.

"What's that?" I asked.

"An oscillator," he answered, without looking up.

"An oscillator, I'm not even sure what that does. But I know it's a little dated."

"You have to start somewhere."

A dog barked. The wind blew. Birds chirped.

The Captain slowly turned his gaze from the oscillator and looked me in the eye. He gave me the same shit-eating grin I'd first seen at my dorm in Stanford. "This thing is going to change the world."

He blinked, and when his eyes opened out streamed a series of computing devices: a calculator, a transistor, a microprocessor, an Apple II, a Walkman, a smartphone...more devices were added to the stream, the flow picked up until it was impossible to identify what each item was.

The Captain blinked again. His eyes returned to normal. His smile vanished. He said, "We're going to make a killing."

33

The next day – seven days after my visit from the Troll – I brought my luggage downstairs to meet Priya by the curb. It was nearly eleven, and I had no doubt that she'd be there on time. No confirmation was required. I travelled light: a shoulder-strap satchel with a small assortment of clothes, a computer bag containing my laptop and iPad mini and augmentation glasses, and a little plastic carrying case that held Magnus. The move didn't seem to bother him, he was sound asleep.

It was the first of October. So October had followed September again, just like it had so many times before.

Priya arrived, as predicted, right on schedule. She was inside a stretch limo, spotlessly clean and painted a celestial shade of white. Behind the wheel was a driver. And since there was no room along the curb for that beast they double parked. A door swung open and I deposited my gear in the long backseat, where Priya sat, and then slid in next to it. She asked about my well-being.

"Great, Priya, just spectacular," I said, which was true. After a restful night's sleep, I woke feeling like a new man. Although I'd been fired (I considered the idea that I was simply on probation to be bullshit), I had a cushy new job that would cover all my expenses and then some, and I'd landed the job with literally no effort. I had been kidnapped and drugged – which logically should have damped my mood – but that seemed like eons ago. Also on the plus side, I'd recently gotten laid for the first time in years, with prospects for more in the future. Yeah, Nika had ignored my texts, but that was only momentarily, I was sure of it.

"Spectacular, you say. I'm glad to hear it." Priya took a sip from a champagne flute, which I just noticed she'd been holding. By the looks of it, the glass contained a mimosa. "Care to join me? I'm not normally one to drink while working, but Mr. Gosling insisted that we have a toast to christen our new business arrangement."

Gosling insisted – so who was I to complain? I was starting to like that old guy more and more. I told her a mimosa sounded great. Priya pulled the necessary ingredients out of the fully stocked bar and concocted my drink. We touched our glasses, sipped. The champagne was Dom Perignon, naturally. I noted its almost perfect quality, and took another, larger sip.

≈≈≈

Gosling's home was in Pacific Heights, on Broadway, in an old money part of San Francisco. It was just a few minutes from my apartment, but worlds away in terms of style. Whereas his Atherton home was relatively modest, his San Francisco abode was a monstrosity. Made of brick and located on a corner lot, the home rested on top of a steep hill. It jutted out of ground like a castle, lording over the smaller homes below it.

"So this is where I'm going to stay?" I asked, wide-eyed, as the driver stopped the limo in the driveway near the front entrance.

"That's right," Priya answered, "come with me."

She waited as I got my bags and then led the way inside. After walking through a foyer, we entered an enormous room; it looked nearly large enough to hold a basketball court. The room was furnished with pricey but comfortable-looking furniture. There was an odd mix of artwork: bronze sculptures, bizarre 3-D holographic paintings, and on one wall hung what I swear was an original Gauguin still life. But the most spectacular feature was the view. The western windows offered a panoramic shot of the San Francisco Bay, scanning all the way from the Golden Gate to the Bay Bridge, Sausalito and Tiburon visible in the distance, and Alcatraz was in the middle, sparkling in its own creepy way.

"This is the main room," said Priya. "The house has two kitchens, six bedrooms, even more bathrooms, and all sorts of others rooms – oh, and an indoor pool in the basement."

"A pool?"

"Yes, a large one. You're free to use it."

"That view is – "

"Otherworldly," she said. Our eyes met and she smiled.

I let Magnus Carlsen out of his cage, patted him on the butt, and encouraged him to explore. "You have lot of room to roam now, little buddy." But ignoring me, he found a chair in the sunlight, settled in, and went back to sleep. Sleep: that was all he ever did.

Priya took me on a tour of the house. Even though she was a predictably economical guide, it still took an hour. The word "house" didn't do it justice. It was a mansion. In addition to the pool, there was a game room and a separate theater with an enormous screen, a library, a greenhouse, and a few other assorted spaces that seemed to have no real purpose. Everything was large and bright and tastefully decorated. As Priya moved from room to room, I tailed behind her, astonished.

"That's all of it," Priya said, once we'd returned to the room where we'd started. "As I said yesterday, Mr. Gosling has other people to look after the home. All you need to do is just live here."

"So why exactly am I needed?"

She shrugged. "That's just the way he is. If he takes a

liking to someone, he hires them. And he can afford it, right? Besides, it seems like a great arrangement for you."

True.

There was an alarm system, which she showed me how to activate, and she said she'd be in touch so they could make arrangements on how to pay me. Then she returned to the limo, leaving Magnus and me to fend for ourselves.

I got a beer out of the fridge. Pulled a chair over next to where Magnus slept. Sat, drank from the bottle, stared out at the view, and said, "We're stepping up in the world, Magnus."

I pulled out my new iPhone and called Nika. She didn't answer and her voicemail box was full, so I couldn't leave a message. I sent another text: *Hi there. Call me, okay?*

≈≈≈

That evening I was stretched out on a sofa reading on my iPad when the doorbell rang. I thought it might be one of the hired cleaners that Priya had mentioned, although 9:00 p.m. did seem rather late to be scrubbing the pool. But when I looked through the peephole I saw two young women. They both wore long trench coats: one black, the other white.

"Can I help you?" I asked, after cracking open the door.

"Hi," said the one in white, "we're tonight's entertainment."

"I didn't hire any entertainment."

"You're friends with a Mr. Gosling, right?"

I told her that I was.

"Then we're at the right spot." There was a pause as I pondered what to do, and then the one in white said, "Well are you going to let us in? It's chilly out here."

So we moved inside.

"I hope we're not disturbing you," said the black-coated one, once we'd entered the main room.

"No, not really, I was just reading."

"Reading what?"

"A Scott Phillips novel."

"Scott Phillips," she parroted, "never heard of him."

Your loss, I thought, but didn't voice.

The woman in white had made her way over to the western windows, and as she looked out she said, "Wow! A person could get used to that view, huh?" She turned to look at me. "You must be one of those dot com millionaires, right?"

I told her not exactly.

"But clearly you're doing okay."

I shrugged. "So do you two have names?"

They each walked toward me, stopped a foot or two away. Both women had hairdos that fell just below their ears and perfectly straight bangs. One had dyed her hair a blinding shade of white, while the other's was dark black. Both sported glossy bright red lipstick.

"I'm Sugar," said the one decked out in all white.

"Of course you are. And that would make you..."

"Spice."

Sugar and Spice: I was starting to get an idea what type of entertainment Gosling had hired for the night.

"Look," I said, "I'm not sure – "

Spice cut me off. "Let's have a drink," she suggested.

That seemed like a good idea. Earlier I'd noticed that there was a bottle of Dom Perignon chilling in the refrigerator (apparently it was Gosling's champagne of choice). I asked the women if champagne would do the trick, and got an enthusiastic yes. I popped it open, and as we drank I made a decision that I wouldn't take advantage of Gosling's offer. Never before had I slept with a hired woman. Not that I was opposed to the practice philosophically, but it was just something I'd hadn't done before. I wasn't about to start. Also, I had a girl friend, or if not officially a girl friend, a woman who I was sleeping with. Nika. It wouldn't be right to have sex with someone else, let alone two women, would it?

And yet once we'd finished our drinks and they dropped their coats and I saw that each wore a skimpy little cleavage accentuating dress – one black, one white, naturally – I started to reconsider.

Sugar licked her lips with the tip of her tongue, grabbed my shirt, and gently pulled me toward her. "You're cute," she said, just before giving me the softest kiss imaginable. While this happened, Spice had moved over to the sofa. She kneeled on the armrest in such a way that her ass was pointed directly at me. Her skirt had hiked up and I could see that she wore no panties. With one hand she slapped her bare ass, hard, and said, "Come get some."

≈≈≈

Legend has it that women hired for sex are not passionate about their work. It's a job, just like any other. They get in, get it done, and get out: wham bam thank you ma'am.

Well, that night I was in for an education. Sugar and Spice approached their tasks with ardor and zeal. I've seen children less eager on Christmas morning. They put me through the paces, twisted me into positions I'd only imagined before, left me so depleted that after a couple of hours I plopped down on the sofa. Magnus, who'd slept through the commotion, took that moment to crack open one eye. He looked my way and then returned back to his dream world. But Sugar and Spice weren't done. No, no, no. They embraced, kissed, Sugar's hand slipped over Spice's breast, while Spice grabbed a handful of Sugar's perfect ass. Watching this got my engines revving again, I reengaged, and the three of us were off and running.

It was past midnight when they finally left.

≈≈≈

I was too amped to sleep.

During my final meeting with the Centre Terrain HR manager, I was informed that I needed to return both the home laptop the company had provided me, and the augmentation glasses. They were company property. At the time I agreed, although I really had no intention of following through. Those assholes could come and get the equipment themselves.

Clearly the Centre Terrain management team had anticipated my attitude, because when I tried to login I found that my password no longer worked. So you think *this* will stop me? I didn't just think it, but actually said those words out loud.

"So you think *this* will stop me?"

It took just a matter of minutes until I'd broken through the security system and was inside the game.

≈≈≈

This time Roma made a point of looking for the big-eyed Halfling and found him almost immediately, just loitering about.

"Back to open the hole?" asked the Halfling.

"That's right."

"Open it, yes, yes, that's right."

He was a weird little dude, but apparently harmless. And Roma actually felt comforted knowing he was there, like the comforting feeling you get when sitting quietly with an old friend.

The hole was still there. Using the caliper, Roma measured it and found that it was the exact same size as before. Then he started coding. This time things went more quickly than before. He'd learned from his previous efforts. When he finished, Roma measured the hole again. It had grown four-tenths of a millimeter. The size of the hole had still barely budged.

"Almost there, almost there," said the Halfling. "It won't be long until you can walk through."

Roma looked at the little guy and just shook his head.

34

The next day I found myself at loose ends. This concerned me. As I've explained, I had a history of going a little off the rails when something is taken away from me. There was chess and then Polpo. I wasn't eager for another occurrence.

Luckily, I didn't have time to wallow in my worry, because early the next morning my phone rang. The caller ID was blocked but I answered anyway. It was Mr. Gosling. He asked what I thought about the house.

"It's spectacular," I said, the understatement of the year.

"I'm glad you like it." He went on to give me a history of the place, which I listened to with half an ear as I nibbled on a banana. Eventually he changed the subject. "So did you get my gift last night?"

Feeling a little squeamish, I told him that I had.

"Did you enjoy it?"

"Uh-huh." That squeamishness morphed into a full-blown discomfort.

"Tell me about it."

"Excuse me?"

"Don't be a prude. Years ago I had cancer and my prostate removed. As a result, I haven't slept with a woman since the Clinton administration. I was a kinky man in my day, a kinky man with unlimited means. But now when it comes to the carnal side of life, I'm forced to live vicariously through others, by proxy, if you will."

I was hit with a powerful feeling of déjà vu, so strong I

felt like I was drowning in it.

There was a long pause as neither of us spoke. It was Gosling who broke the quiet. "All right then, out with it."

So I let him have it, both barrels. I spilled my guts like a sorority girl, spared none of the juicy details, didn't embellish – there was no need to – but informed him about the dirty talk and the sexy visuals, the girl-on-girl play and the many assorted positions. I told him everything.

"Well, well," he said when I'd finished. "Now that's something now, isn't it? Yes, something indeed. You did well son."

"Thanks, I guess."

We talked a bit longer. He thanked me for looking after his home, the call ended.

≈≈≈

Soon after, Priya rang. I had moved outside to the balcony where I was relaxing on a lounge chair, soaking in the view and eating an Asian pear. She wanted to know if everything was okay, if I needed anything else. I told her I was fine, couldn't be better. She asked how my first night went, and I said it had been quiet. She accepted this without commentary, which I took to mean that Gosling hadn't instructed Priya to arrange my nighttime visitors – a fact that I appreciated.

"If I get a chance, I'll stop by and see how you're doing," she said.

I told her that would be fine.

≈≈≈

It was my turn to phone someone. I dialed up Whitfield.

"Keemosabee," he said. "Long time no talk. Sorry I haven't been in touch. I've been out of town. Just got in last night."

"No worries. The phone works both ways. I could have

contacted you."

"True." Pause. "So how's life?"

"Better than the alternative."

"Ouch. Do I gather that things are not well in your world?"

"No, no. Things are good. A lot has happened, though."

"Such as..."

I recapped everything: getting fired, kidnapped, my meeting with Roderick Jaynes, the hallucination, my phone getting stolen, Priya's visit, her job offer, and finally working for Gosling. When it was all condensed liked that it seemed like a lot of water had rushed under the bridge.

"Wow," he said, once I'd finished. "That's some crazy shit."

"Yeah."

"So you met Roderick Jaynes?"

I had, I said.

"You know who he is, right?"

I told him that I didn't know anything about Jaynes, outside of what he'd had told me at his office.

Whitfield sighed. "You really are clueless sometimes. Is it okay if I shed some light?"

"Go ahead..."

"Jaynes represents a man known as the General. He's a real big swinging dick."

"The General?"

"That's right. That's what he calls himself. Although in truth, he has no military background. Zero. He gave himself the moniker to lend an air of respectability."

"Respectability? I thought he was a venture capitalist."

"He is. But he didn't start out that way. He made his fortune in the porn industry. Back in the early 1970s, when movies like *Deep Throat* were becoming popular, the General launched a chain of porn-centric movie theaters throughout the country. He did well and branched out by opening strip clubs, real hardcore places with lap dances and raunchy stage shows and special green door rooms."

Whitfield paused, and it sounded like he was taking a hit off a joint.

He continued, his voice a little gravelly: "And then the General expanded further. He created a line of hardcore porn magazines, real smut. Smut sells. And by the start of the 90s, he'd created a business empire worth billions. And that's when he started branching into technology."

"He became a venture capitalist..."

"Exactly. As the Internet started to take off, the General was one of the first investors to see the opportunity to sell porn online. He made billions on top of his billions. It wasn't until the end of the 90s that he started to invest in technologies outside of porn, and when he did he went in whole hog. He was a serious player in the dot com boom. But, the General he didn't just invest in start-ups. He also purchased existing companies, specializing in acquiring troubled firms, firing the employees, and selling the assets.

"He has no interest creating anything. The one thing that matters to him is making money. He's practically demonic when it comes to maximizing profits. If the General is interested in the Troll, then this could be bigger than I thought."

The conversation lulled as I let what Whitfield told me sink in.

"Have you met the General?" I asked, eventually.

"No, I haven't. But I have seen him lurking about at trade shows. Rumor has it that he splits his time between an enormous penthouse in San Francisco, and the world's largest yacht that he keeps docked in the Mediterranean."

"Hey," Whitfield said, shifting gears abruptly, "so you're at Gosling's home right now? And it's right on

Billionaire's Row?"

Yes and yes, I told him.

"I'd like to see that home. And I have an idea."

"Swing on by."

I gave him the address and he said he'd be right over.

≈≈≈

Not much later, Whitfield arrived at Gosling's house. I was struck by how good it felt to see him. Whitfield always brightened my mood.

As he walked in the door and through the foyer and into the main room, he said, "So this is how the other half lives,"

"The other half? Try the one percent."

"True. That's true, brother, that's true."

When he got an eyeful of the view he started cackling. "Ha ... ha ... haaaa!" He smiled, a little fiendishly. "Let's get high and hang out on the patio."

We stepped outside and in no time we were cooked. And that's when Whitfield sprung his idea.

"Last week I wrote a short news blurb, just a couple of paragraphs, with information on a new programmer that Roderick Jaynes had hired for the General's organization. It was newsworthy for a few of reasons." Whitfield held up a thumb. "First," he said, "the programmer was given an ungodly signing bonus. Over three hundred thousand dollars. Second..." his index finger shot up, "...it's more than a little unusual for a venture capitalist firm to hire a programmer directly. Especially one that costs that much. And third..." out came the middle-finger, "...the programmer negotiated a special working relationship. He hates offices, so works exclusively at home. Or more precisely, at a coffee shop. That's where he goes every day."

"And you think this programmer is tied to the Troll?"

"Bingo. It makes sense, right? You were visited by the

Troll, Jaynes knew about it, and then the programmer was hired. His name is Jason Loo, by the way."

"The programmer?"

"That's right."

"Okay. So what? What are you proposing?"

"We steal Loo's laptop and see what he's working on."

Steal his laptop. That struck me as a lame-brained idea. "That's crazy. We could end up in jail for that."

Whitfield snorted. "Don't be melodramatic," he said. "At worst, we'd have to pay a small fine."

That seemed suspect, but I went with it. "Okay. Let's assume it is a good idea. How do you propose we pull off this heist?"

He paused for a minute, just long enough to take one more hit off what was left of the joint we'd been smoking. As smoke streamed out his nose he said, "The coffee shop where Loo works is in Pacific Heights, on Fillmore, just a few blocks from here." He dropped what was left of the joint on Gosling's patio and rubbed it out with his shoe. "I'll tell you my plan when we get there."

≈≈≈

Less than fifteen minutes later we arrived at the coffee shop. It had large windows on the front wall, all of which were pulled open so that it felt like the place was as much outdoors as indoors. It was jammed with people. Whitfield and I hovered outside on the sidewalk and peered inside.

"That's him," Whitfield said, pointing discreetly at a young man sitting alone in the corner of the café. "That's Loo."

I sized him up. He had short black hair and a bright red birthmark on one side of his face. He was typing on a laptop, engrossed in whatever he was doing.

I looked at Whitfield. "Okay. That's him. So what's your plan? We go over there, hit him on the head, grab his laptop, and make a run for it."

Whitfield frowned. "Don't be snide. No. We give him this."

Out of his shirt pocket Whitfield pulled a small, square piece of paper.

"So what's that?" I asked.

'It's acid. LSD," Whitfield said, in a hushed tone.

"Jeez. So you want to drug him?"

"Yes. That's exactly what I want to do. Don't be such a pussy. Jaynes drugged you, right? It seems only fair to return the favor."

He did have something of a point.

"This shit is made by my same friends who designed the weed I gave you. Ten minutes after swallowing this and Loo over there will be seeing bugs crawling on the walls."

I nodded. "Okay. So how do we get him to eat it?"

"We walk over there, you make some type of distraction, and when Loo's turns his head I drop this square into his coffee. Easy."

That did sound easy enough. But I still wasn't convinced.

"You want to learn more about the Troll, right?" Whitfield asked. I nodded. "Well, then, here's your chance. Unless you have a better idea...."

I didn't. So after a little more coaxing I gave in and we followed Whitfield's plan, just as he had spelled it out. I walked near where Loo was sitting, stumbled into some chairs, made a loud racket, Loo looked in my direction, and out of the corner of my eye I saw Whitfield drop the square into Loo's mug.

Afterward, Whitfield and I each ordered a cup of coffee, sat near Loo, and waited.

It didn't take long. Soon Loo's head was cast upwards, with both hands he appeared to be grabbing at imaginary objects flying around him. By the look on his face, an elephant could have walked past him and Loo wouldn't have noticed.

Whitfield walked over to where Loo was sitting and pretended to engage him in a conversation. Then in one smooth motion Whitfield leaned over, snatched up the laptop, and proceeded to head to the front door. No one in the coffee shop so much as batted an eye.

≈≈≈

Back at Gosling's I logged into Loo's computer. I didn't have the password, but that was easy enough for me to work around. As I did so Whitfield looked over my shoulder. Once inside, on the computer's desktop was a folder called, "Work for the General."

"Pay dirt!" Whitfield said, gleefully.

I clicked open the folder. Inside was just one file. Loo had titled it "X." It was an AVI file, a video. I clicked on that.

Whitfield and I watched as the video ran. It was a cartoon, extremely high quality, the best I'd seen.

"I forgot to mention," Whitfield said, "that one of Loo's specialties is animation."

I nodded. The video continued to run. An animated woman appeared wearing a skin-tight tank top and equally tight Daisy Dukes. Another cartoon woman entered the scene. She was also skimpily dressed. The two women embraced, kissed, removed their clothes, and were soon engaged in an assortment of provocative sex acts.

I glanced back at Whitfield. "It looks like porn," I said.

"Hmmm..." he grunted.

I fast forwarded. More animated sex scenes. The quality was spectacular, but it didn't strike me as what the Troll was after.

"It looks to me like the General hired Loo to help with his online porn business," I said. "I don't think this has anything to do with the Troll."

Whitfield stood up and cracked a knuckle. He nodded

a few times and then said, "You're right. Well, that didn't work out as I'd hoped." He paused for a beat and then said, "Let's get stoned."

35

Since my experiment in crime with Whitfield had proven to be an utter failure, the next day I decided that the first order of business was to create a file with everything I'd uncovered so far on the Troll. I'd read enough detective novels to know that was the way things were done. But I didn't have anything to put in a folder, not a photograph or medical records or banking history. Nada, zip, zero. For that matter, I didn't have the folder itself. I could have dug into Gosling's drawers and probably found a pen and a pad of paper, but instead I opened the email app in my iPad and using bullet points came up with this list:

- Tall (7 feet)
- Genius
- Into computers (mostly hardware)
- Played high school basketball (less than one year)
- Prolific reader
- Designed neural processor
- Co-founder of Centre Terrain
- Interested in Quantum Mechanics
- Spent time alone in seedy hotel (Nika's dreams)
- Told me that together we'd change the world
- Ugly as all get out (according to Gosling, but I'd seen him and thought he looked cool, in a funky way)
- Never been seen (at least not by anyone that I knew – except myself, through my processor)

- Nika and the General/Roderick Jaynes are interested in him
- The Troll gives me a sense of belonging.

When I finished I poured myself into studying the text hoping that somehow the simple act of jotting down this paltry amount of information would jog a reaction in my brain, unlock a clue that would help me get closer to the Troll. It didn't. Nothing popped into my head except the thought that I'd make a terrible private detective, hardboiled, white gloved, or otherwise. There seemed to be some clues: I'd been visited by the Troll, Nika had seen the Troll in her dreams. But I'd be damned if I could make heads or tails of it. Nothing made sense.

"It's a tough nut to crack," I said to Magnus Carlsen, who, predictably, was half asleep on the sofa.

The sound of my voice spurred Magnus to open his eyes. He raised his head and said, "Meow." When I didn't respond, he said it again, "Meow, Meow, Meow!" Clearly, he had a point he was trying to get across.

"Sorry, Magnus, I wish I could understand you."

I'll be damned if the little guy didn't shrug and then sink into his seat on the sofa.

At that moment, just like that, something started to bubble up in my brain. I could feel it moving around, climbing to the surface, but before it could break free it dissolved into the void of unknowable ideas.

I decided that getting high might help, spur on my creative juices. I dug a few of the vials that Whitfield had given me out of my luggage and rolled ten fat joints (I'd need some for later). I smoked an entire joint. It didn't help. Does it ever really help accomplish anything, besides just getting buzzed?

≈≈≈

Another fruitless task behind me, I decided to go for a

walk, clear my head. After donning a jacket I walked south, just killing time, no specific destination in mind, past a string of mansions that stretched along Broadway, most with driveways populated with either a shiny Jaguar or Bentley or Mercedes, until I arrived at a cement staircase on Lyon Street that led downhill toward Cow Hollow.

I rambled down, going west. Both sides of the staircase were lined with perfectly manicured hedges. The day was moist, foggy. San Francisco fog burrows under the skin, digs into the bones, makes you feel like you'll never be warm again. I zipped my jacket up until it was cinched right under my chin. My hands plunged deep into my pockets. Still, even with the nip in the air, it was a good day for walking; San Francisco is a great walking city. Once at the bottom of the stairs my pace quickened. I hurried through Cow Hollow into the Marina and eventually made it all the way to the edge of the water. During the walk the fog had thickened, so much so that it was impossible to see more than dozen feet ahead. The temp had morphed from nippy to frigid. The wind kicked up its heels. An old woman fed breadcrumbs to some seagulls. But she was made of stouter stuff than I. I turned around and headed back inland, walked aimlessly, my eyes focused on the sidewalk, the streets empty of pedestrians, the wind pushing gum wrappers through the air, until somehow or other I found myself standing in front of a red doorway with a sign that read: *Lost Tribe, Tattoo Parlor.*

I stood there for a minute, considered the sign, then opened the door and stepped through.

Inside there was a man that I assumed was the tattoo artist. He had a beard and long, wild hair. He had freaky tattoos that ran up the length of his arms, like sleeves. He was working on the deltoid of a young woman, needle to skin.

"Can I help you," he asked. He gave me a perfunctory

glance before returning to his work.

"I'd like to get a tattoo." The words leapt from my mouth, as if sprung from a cage, although the thought had never occurred to me before that very moment.

He stopped what he was doing, sized me up more closely. He ran his eyes from my feet to my head, and said, "Are you sure? You don't look the type."

I told him I was sure.

"All right. I'm almost done. Come back in an hour. We'll talk."

As soon as I left I could feel my courage ebb. Luckily, there was a bar right next door. I sat on one of the stools and knocked back two Bloody Marys. Using my iPhone, I went online and read Yelp! reviews on the tattoo parlor. Two phrases – "very clean" and "top notch artist" – leapt off the screen, and I decided to proceed. I ordered one more Bloody Mary, borrowed a pen from the bartender, and on a cocktail napkin scribbled down the design I wanted.

When I returned to the tattoo parlor the artist was alone. Without smiling he asked, "Do you have a design in mind?"

"I do." I gave him the napkin.

He examined it. "This is binary code, right?" he asked.

It's my name, I told him.

He grunted. "Whatever rocks your boat. This shouldn't take long," he said, meaning the design. "I can squeeze you in."

He had me select a font for the numbers. I told him I wanted it small, about two-inches long, and on the inside of my right forearm. What I didn't tell him is that I wanted it to closely resemble the binary code that I'd seen floating around the Troll, the night he'd visited me.

The process took longer and was more painful than I'd anticipated. My head was heavy from the weed and vodka.

As he worked an image of Nika with the Troll flashed through my mind. I saw them standing at a computer keyboard, Nika typing as the Troll relayed instructions. As I observed, Nika pulled her eyes away from the computer screen, she smiled, blew me a kiss.

When the artist finished I felt woozy, close to vomiting.

"Do we need to wrap it in a gauze bandage?" I asked.

"No. Just keep it out of the sun."

I paid and was out the door.

I walked back to Gosling's place, up the steep hill toward Pacific Heights, my head feeling increasingly muddy with each step. It occurred to me that I'd neglected to eat that day. When I finally arrived at the mansion my legs felt like two noodles, my dogs barked. I drank a glass of water and stuffed a handful of grapes into my mouth, hoping they would help to right the ship. They didn't. I took a few steps toward the sofa but couldn't make it, curled up in a ball, and passed out on the floor.

36

Almost immediately I was visited by the Troll. This time around I knew it wasn't a dream, I'd been down that faulty path before. I suppose it's not really accurate to say that the Troll visited me; it was more like I was transported to his location. He was inside an enormous server farm. Rectangular computers, black and silver, each over seven-feet tall, stretched into infinity: row after row after row. The room was frigid, the computers hummed. The Troll wore a white lab coat that stretched down below his knees. He was fiddling with the servers, doing God knows what. He looked more serious than before, determined, a few extra lines etched across his forehead.

I walked slowly toward him and as I did I was hit by the strength of his charisma, just like Nika said she had been in her dreams. It was overpowering, a living thing in the room. Something sparked in me, I felt alive with possibility.

"You returned," I said.

He spun, faced my direction, and bestowed on me his undivided attention. "You've been asking questions about me," he said.

Startled, I just nodded. Although I felt good, the same feeling of belonging that had hit me before swept over me again. Apparently the Troll had that impact on me.

"Have you come to any conclusions?" he asked.

"Not really."

"You'll get there. Just keep doing what you're doing."

"What am I doing?"

No response. The computers kept right on humming. The chill in the room was starting to get to me and I wished I had a sweater.

The Troll stepped toward me, looked at my right arm. "You got a tattoo, I see."

I nodded.

We each looked at the tattoo, examined it closely, and watched as the blue numbers appeared to glow. Time seemed to grind to a halt.

Eventually the Troll spoke. "It's cool. I approve."

"Can I ask a question?"

"Sure," he replied.

"You said we were going to change the world, what exactly did you mean?"

He smiled, slyly. "I can't tell you, at least not yet. You need to figure it out on your own."

"Why?"

He shrugged. "I will tell you that you're making progress."

"I am?"

"Uh-huh."

"How? What kind of progress? You talk in riddles, why is that?"

He smiled that same sly grin. "Why is the sky blue? Why do birds sing? Why do little girls blush?"

More riddles. Maybe that's just the way it is with trolls, or at least this particular one.

I gathered he could tell that I was getting frustrated because he threw me a bone. "You know what you need to do next, right?"

I examined my subconscious, really dug inside, and realized he was right, I did know what I needed to do. I just wasn't ready to cross that bridge, not quite yet.

"So how does this all play out?" I asked.

"What do you mean?" he seemed genuinely puzzled by

the question.

"What's the endgame? At some point you'll offer me something, something I really want, and in exchange I give you my soul, right?"

The Troll was taken aback. "This isn't a fairy tale."

"It's not?"

"No. Of course not. This is real life. I'm not going to be offering you anything, at least not in the sense that you're thinking. I need something from *you*. And I need you to get there on your own. I can only help so much."

There was a long silence as the Troll let me process what he'd said, let it settle in. When he did eventually speak he said, "There is something else I need to tell you."

"Oh yeah?" I asked.

He frowned. "You're not going to like it." Pause. "But here is it...I took your friend?"

"Didn't we cover that already?"

"No. Nika."

Nika – what the *fuck*? He was right: I didn't like it, not one little bit. I saw red, although it did explain her disappearance.

"Now don't get all huffy," he said, in response to my demeanor. "Saying I took her isn't exactly right. She volunteered to go. She's a little ahead of you, on the work, that is. She's already working on the program I need. If you think you're the real deal, then you have some catching up to do." He smiled. "It's all business, I'm sure you can appreciate that."

"What do you mean? She's ahead of me how? Where did you take her?" I blurted out, but I don't think he heard me. The scene faded, enveloped in black, and I drifted off to a dream.

37

I woke up disoriented. My back ached. It took me a moment to realize I was still stretched out on the floor. But there was a pillow under my head and I was covered by a blanket, a big comforter. My eyes took their own sweet time to adjust – everything was blurry, out of focus – but it finally cleared and I could make out my surroundings.

In the distance I saw the kitchen, the stairs that led to the second floor, the expensive paintings on the wall, a sofa. On the sofa was a human figure. I shook my head, cleared out the cobwebs, until my mind registered who it was. Priya. She sat on the edge of the cushion, legs crossed, her right foot dangled and spun in a slow circle. With one hand she gently stroked between the ears of a purring Magnus Carlsen.

"Priya?"

"I tried to move you," she said, "but you were too heavy. So I just gave you the blanket and a pillow."

"How long have I been out?" I pushed myself up onto an elbow.

"Hard to tell. I've been here over three hours and you've been out the whole time. I don't think an earthquake would have roused you. I fed your cat." Magnus started to purr even louder.

"You did. That's great. Thank you. For the blanket, the pillow, Magnus. For everything. Really." I was then struck with an overwhelming need to pee. I excused myself and dashed off the can. When I returned Priya was still lodged on the sofa.

"I see you got a tattoo," she said.

By the look on her face I couldn't tell if she approved. Her expression was caught halfway between sardonic and amused.

I rubbed my fingers lightly over the tattoo. There was no swelling, no irritation. It looked good.

"I got it today. At least I think it was today."

"I hope I'm not being rude, but you don't look well. You're gaunt. And your skin is a little orangey."

I told her that I'd barely eaten all day, just a few grapes.

She shook her head, frowned. "That's not good for you." Then she stood up. "Come on," she said, "let's go get dinner."

"Where to?"

"I'll tell you in the car."

I followed her as she led the way to the front door. Something in me sparked, brightened, I could feel myself breathe easier.

≈≈≈

Outside it was nighttime, the sky clear, a full moon. Priya had a sporty two-door BMW. We drove across the Golden Gate Bridge toward Marin. On the ride over Priya told me about her MBA program and what she'd been doing with Mr. Gosling.

"He definitely keeps me hopping," she said, as she steered us into the parking lot.

I listened but was preoccupied. My mind kept drifting back to what the Troll had told me.

She's already working on the program I need. It's all business.

So was Nika a competitor of mine? And what was the deal with Jaynes?

Priya pulled into a parking lot for a restaurant named,

The Buckeye Roadhouse. We pulled to a stop and she turned off the ignition.

Once inside the restaurant, we decided to eat at the bar. Priya ordered a dozen oysters bingo which she insisted I split with her. She got a martini, but I opted for just a tall glass of water. I ordered a thick, bloody steak, with green beans and mashed potatoes. After dinner we split a piece of chocolate cake. My stomach was full, happy. I felt good, damn good, better than I had a right to.

Back outside the air had cooled. The moon had risen higher into the sky.

As we walked toward Priya's car I saw that something was on top of its roof, something alive, standing. The BMW was tucked away in the corner of the parking lot, far from the lights, so at first I couldn't determine what it was. But as we moved closer I could see that is was a bird: a tall, thin, crane. It was completely white except for its beak which was black and orange. The bird's head was pointed skyward and I followed the line of its gaze. It appeared to be studying the moon, examining its glowing nimbus.

Priya and I slowed our pace but kept walking until we were almost close enough to the car so that we could touch the door handles. A frog croaked. I moved my eyes from the bird to the moon and back again. Then I looked over at Priya. She was staring at the bird as well, her face calm, expressionless, but her eyes unwavering, fixated.

"I think this is a good omen," I whispered out of the side of my mouth. "Like finding a lady bug. Or the opposite of seeing a black cat."

I couldn't tell if Priya had heard me because she didn't respond, not right away. But after a minute or so she whispered back, "There are no omens."

The bird took that moment to shift its gaze toward us. It adjusted its position slightly, its talons softly clicking on the car's roof. It lowered its head and used its long neck to stretch toward us. If it knew how, I bet that darn bird would have winked. Instead, it spread its wings, stretched them to their maximum extension. It flapped, took flight, escaped from the car. We watched as it glided over some trees and off toward the bay until it got so small we could no longer see it.

I looked back at Priya. Even though the crane was no longer visible her eyes stayed glued to a spot in the distance, transfixed, as if she could make out something that I couldn't.

≈≈≈

The roads were nearly empty on the drive back. As we sped over the bridge I could make out just a few boats on the bay; the city lights twinkled.

During the ride I kept thinking about the crane.

"Have you ever seen anything like that?" I asked Priya. "A bird, on the roof, I mean."

She steered using only her right hand. Her left arm, which was bent at the elbow, rested on top of her open window.

"I've seen a lot of cranes, but never one standing on top of my car."

"And you don't believe in omens?"

She chortled and then stifled it. "Omens. No. People used to dream up all sorts of stories to explain weird occurrences – eclipses, tornadoes, other natural disasters. The Gods were angry with them so they handed out punishment. But we have science now. We can explain how and why things happen."

She looked at me. Her eyes widened, as if she were gazing into the galactic unknown.

"The bird had probably chased some insects up onto the roof of the car, and then got attracted by the glow of the moon."

"You're probably right," I conceded. But I wasn't

buying it, not for a second.

≈≈≈

When we arrived at Gosling's house I invited Priya to join me for a nightcap, but she told me that she had to leave.

Inside the home was quiet, eerily so. It was also dark, so I flipped on some lights. I wondered if Gosling had ever actually lived in the home, or even used it, for that matter.

"Magnus," I called out, "where are you?" No response. "Magnus, come here." I went searching for him. I checked my bedroom first, but he wasn't there. I was aware of a few other haunts where I knew he tended to frequent, but after checking each one I came up empty. Somehow or other I found myself in Gosling's library. The room was gigantic: shaped like an oval, bookcases that rose up to the high ceiling, no windows except a large, round skylight. There was a ladder with wheels on the bottom that you could push around the room and climb up to get to the books at the top. I've always loved libraries; the sense they gave me that I am surrounded by knowledge. It struck me that I wasn't currently reading a book, so I decided to see what Gosling had to offer.

I circled the bookcases, ran my fingers along the bindings, read the titles. Some of the books were caked with dust, obviously not touched or cleaned in years. The room smelled like ammonia, just a hint of it. Someone had organized the books into sections. There was science and technology, history and memoirs, architecture and sports. Gosling had a large collection of detective novels, dog-eared paperbacks. He had the classics – books written by Chandler and Hammett and Spillane – but also one penned by James Crumley and two by Sara Gran, which I thought was cool. I leafed through one of the Gran novels, read a couple of chapters, considered taking it back to the main room and settling down for the day, but then decided not to and slipped it back into its spot. It was a gripping read, but I was in the mood for something else.

So I took two big steps and landed at the biography section. Right at eye level was a book called *Steve Jobs*, written by Walter Isaacson. By its dust-free cover, I gathered that someone had read it recently. I knew the basic parameters of Jobs' life story — it was nearly impossible to work in Silicon Valley and not know it. But I wasn't familiar with the details. I slipped the tome out of its spot, walked upstairs, got ready for bed, and climbed under the covers. I read the Jobs bio, and made it far enough into it to learn about some of Jobs' youthful peculiarities: a fruit-only diet, an unwillingness to shower for days at a time, a quest to India to find his "guru," and experimentation with weed, acid, and other drugs. It was spellbinding. But before I could go any further I started to lose focus. So I let my head sink into the pillow. I felt something jump up onto the foot of the bed and heard Magnus let out a soft meow. In no time, I drifted off to sleep.

That night I didn't dream, not a single one.

38

Roma arrived in the field of mushrooms to find it had grown, it had grown substantially. Coders had been busy, adding lines to the program, expanding the level so it seemed to stretch on and on with no end in sight. More mushrooms, butterflies of all shapes filled the sky.

There were some characters this time as well. A small group of humanoids, humans and elves, congregated around a small bonfire and hypnotically watched sparks escape from the flames and float upward. Roma walked past them, along a narrow rabbit path. After a dozen feet he encountered a lone male character, a longhaired hippie, slowly spinning in a circle and looking skyward. The hippie stood right smack dab in the center of the path. Roma tried to skirt around him.

"Dude, eat the mushrooms," the hippie said, and grabbed Roma by the arm. "You'll get the answers, man."

Roma tugged his arm free, but the character grabbed it again, squeezed tightly. Roma looked around and saw that the group seated around the campfire was watching the scene.

The hazy expression on the hippie's face cleared a little. "Hey," he said. "You're one of those Sweepers, right?" His grip grew tighter. Roma could have killed him with a flick of a finger. He didn't. Instead, Roma tugged his arm free and kept walking, but the hippie re-grabbed his arm and said, "Do something cool."

Roma broke free again. "Not today," was all he said, and hurried down the path. He glanced back to see that the hippie had resumed his methodical twirling.

The path got wider. A light drizzle began to fall, stayed with Roma for half an hour before clearing. There were no other characters around; nothing except the mushrooms and the butterflies.

Then a rainbow filled the sky. A small clearing emerged in the field of mushrooms. Two women – one old, one middle-aged – stood in the middle. The older woman popped tiny mushrooms into the other's mouth. "What you'll see is the truth," the old woman said. "The plant will hit your system and push away the clouds until all is known. Although not known in a way that things are easily known, but known in a way where it's there but you still need to decipher the meaning. And the colors and the lights will help guide the way."

Okay...

Roma strode past and the women ignored him. The old one continued to spout gibberish.

Twenty minutes later a fork appeared in the path and on instinct Roma chose the rightward way. Of course, all the walking was unnecessary. Roma would have simply materialized in the spot where the hole in the program resided, which was where he was heading. But he was in a walking mood. After a few more twists and turns another clearing appeared and Roma recognized it as his destination.

Sitting cross-legged on the ground near the edge of the clearing was the big-eyed Halfling.

"There you are," the Halfling said. "You look exhausted."

Roma sat down next to the little guy.

"Have you returned to open the hole?" the Halfling asked. "*Hmmmaaa...*"

"Not today. I just came to visit. I needed a change of scenery."

"That's too bad. You're getting so close, closer every time. You need to keep at it."

Roma chose to ignore the comment. "I'm trying to find someone," he offered. "The Troll."

"A troll, really," the Halfling said, almost too quickly. "There are lots of trolls around here, trolls wherever you look."

"I'm looking for a particular Troll."

The Halfling picked a stick up off the ground and used it to dig a little hole in the dirt. As Roma sat with the Halfling he was struck with a vexing feeling, like an itch in the middle of his back that his thumb couldn't quite reach. He was struck by the same feeling of familiarity that he'd felt before.

"He took my girlfriend," Roma said. "You've seen her. Jett. The Sweeper who killed all those Orcs, back the day you and I met."

The Halfling continued to dig into the ground, using more force until the stick snapped in two.

"Jett – I haven't seen her," that Halfling said. "Not since that day. And I don't know anything about a specific Troll." Roma fixed his eyes right on the Halfling's face. The odd little guy squirmed, seemingly made uncomfortable by the force of Roma's glare.

The Halfling was lying. It was clear to Roma. The little guy's entire demeanor was a charade. But Roma decided to let it go, shifted his eyes away. He stood, walked toward the hole, pulled out the caliper, and measured it. It was the exact same size as before.

"Good, good," the Halfling said, "back to opening the hole." His eyes did a weird little dance and he said, "*Hmmmaaa...*" again.

"Not today. I'm really focused on finding the Troll I mentioned. And I've made almost no progress. It's discouraging."

The Halfling's face took on a frustrated expression. "The hole," he said. "The hole, the hole, the hole..." He kept repeating it, over and over, like a mantra.

39

The next day I called Whitfield and invited him back to Gosling's house.

Together we raided the refrigerator. Priya must have arranged to have someone shop recently, because the pantries were stocked. We loaded up on goodies. We each got a beer, moved outside to the lounge chairs. Whitfield lit a joint and we passed it back and forth. It was another perfect day: warm, cloudless, no fog on the horizon.

For a long time we didn't talk. Thoughts of the Troll seemed to linger in the air, but we didn't discuss him or what had happened with Jason Loo. Instead, I simply enjoyed my buzz, the sun on my face, the jaw-dropping view. It was quiet, weirdly so, considering we were inside a major American city. But Gosling's house was a sanctuary, removed from the commotion.

Eventually, Whitfield broke the silence.

"I have some news." He sat up a little in his chair.

I glanced his way. "Oh yeah?"

"I got an advance on a book deal."

"That's great. What's it about?"

"I'm going to profile ten tech innovators, some of the people who laid the foundation for the Valley. But not the normal names – Packard, Noyce, Jobs. No. I'm going to look at lesser known people, real hardcore engineers, people who got their hands dirty."

"That's awesome," I said.

Over the years, Whitfield had fostered a reputation as a reporter who really understood technology, who was interested in explaining to his audience how things worked. He was more than just the run-of-the-mill newshound. Whitfield delved into the nitty-gritty underworking's of what made the Valley tick. The book he outlined sounded right up his alley.

"I've already started researching it, done a few interviews. And, interestingly, I found one thing that all these men have in common."

"Oh yeah, what's that?"

"As kids, each one took apart their family's radios so they could examine it and learn how the thing worked."

Just like Gosling, I thought, but didn't say.

This nugget of information elicited real joy in Whitfield. For the next twenty minutes, I listened as he excitedly told me about his project.

≈≈≈

The sun sunk below the Marin Headlands, the air cooled, and Whitfield and I moved into the house.

We got two more beers, and then he said, "Let's check out the theater you told me about."

The room actually looked like a movie theater, with three rows of seats, although the chairs were more comfortable than what's typically offered. The screen came down from the ceiling, the movies projected onto it.

I selected a chair up front while Whitfield looked through Gosling's library of movies.

"Lots of older stuff," said Whitfield, "classics." He rattled through a series of titles, discarded one movie after a next, until he landed on one that seemed to hit his fancy. "*Vertigo*, God, I haven't watched this movie in forever."

"I've never seen it."

He stared at me, incredulous. "You're kidding?"

I told him I wasn't.

"Well you're in for a treat. It's brilliant, my friend, especially if you live in San Francisco."

Whitfield cued up the DVD and he settled into a seat near mine. About twenty minutes into the movie I heard snoring and looked over and found Whitfield fast asleep, slumped low in his chair. I left him alone.

The movie was fantastic. When it finished I jostled Whitfield awake, and as he came to he said, "What, oh, wait." He rubbed his head, cleared his throat. "I wasn't sleeping, just resting my eyes."

I let the comment go.

Not much later we were outside, in front of the house. We hugged and I watched as he got into his car and drove off.

I was famished. I whipped up a sandwich, found a bag of potato chips, chowed down.

As I ate my mind drifted to Whitfield. I'd known him just a short time, but we'd developed a strong bond, as if we'd somehow been connected before. I was lucky to have him as a friend. I pictured him from earlier in that afternoon, outside, on Gosling's patio. The day was crisp. A soft, moist breeze blew in from the Pacific. Far in the distance, sunlight reflected off the Golden Gate Bridge; gently residing below it was water – half bay, half ocean, azure and lovely.

Whitfield told me about the book he was to write. A satisfied expression had stolen over his face. His hair was a wild mess. In his right hand he held a half-smoked joint, which he used as a pointing device, thrusting it toward me when he wanted to emphasize something. He looked so alive, vibrant, and even younger, as if his new project was working to melt away some of the years he'd accumulated. He talked and I listened and the world seemed right.

≈≈≈

The next day, Whitfield was dead.

40

"Do you like jazz?" Whitfield asked me one night, two months after we'd first met. I'd arrived at his home for another round of smoking and chess playing, but he had other ideas.

"Not really, I've never gotten into it. It just seems to jump around."

Whitfield shook his head.

"Well, my young friend," he said, "it's high time we set you straight." He waved two tickets that he held in his right hand. "One of my former colleagues gave these to me, prime seats to a little jazz club. The show starts late tonight. Can I talk you into joining me?"

"Sure, why not."

We piled into Whitfield's ancient Volvo and crossed the Bay Bridge. We landed first at a tiny New Orleans-style restaurant in Oakland. The air so spicy it stung your eyes. We ordered red beans and rice, gumbo and collard greens, and an assortment of other Cajun goodies. The food was crazy delicious.

"If anyone should appreciate jazz," Whitfield said as he ate a cornbread muffin, "it's you."

"Oh yeah, why's that?"

"It's like chess."

I offered up a quizzical look.

"You don't know how a game is going to play out when you start, right?" He didn't pause long enough for me to respond. "No, man, of course not, it's impossible to map out an entire game. But you have a general sense of where it's going. And you rely on instinct and intuition to guide you to what to do next. And the more you play the better that intuition becomes. Jazz is just like that, man, just like that. You gotta feel your way along."

I could see what he was getting at.

"Do you play an instrument?" I asked.

"No. I don't have the aptitude for it. But my brother, he blows a horn."

Whitfield spent the rest of the meal telling me about his family.

≈≈≈

The jazz club was close to downtown Oakland, in a sketchy part of town, but the building itself was nice. It had a warm and reddish vibe, a welcoming glow. Inside it was dimly lit. There were two levels, separated in height by just a few feet. Both were populated with round tables that sat two people. The drinks flowed, the crowd buzzed. It was the type of joint that I imagined would have been smoke filled back in the days before public smoking was outlawed in California.

Whitfield and I were escorted to a reserved table a few feet from a small stage where a three-piece band was already strumming and wailing. As soon as we sat Whitfield closed his eyes and tapped his foot to the music. I watched the band play, got drunk on whiskeys and Cokes, soaked in the atmosphere.

We shut the place down.

I passed out in his car on the ride home. Not knowing where I lived, Whitfield took me to his house, practically dragged me inside, and for the first time let me crash on his sofa.

The next day I told him, "I get your point now, about jazz, I mean."

"I knew you'd see the light."

We smiled at each other.

Was it an epic night out? No, not really. But it laid a solid plank on the foundation of our friendship. And maybe like a lot of people, I could count the number of real friends that I'd had on one hand, or even just a couple of fingers.

And then Whitfield was gone. And Nika was with the Troll. And I felt all alone.

41

Whitfield died from heart failure. It turned out he had an abnormality, a birth defect with one of his valves that could have been remedied with a pacemaker. Death came immediately, and the doctors informed his family that he'd felt no pain.

His sister called me and delivered the horrible news. I'd just finished a morning swim and was feeling sprightly as I started into a cup of coffee. I'd planned to spend the day just loafing, carefree. The news of Whitfield's death hit me like a punch in the gut. I said almost nothing as his sister spoke, but was able to express my deep sorrow and sympathy for the family.

Once I'd hung up I went to the sink and puked out the entire contents of my stomach. My mind had processed what had happened, but my body rejected it. I was the last person to see Whitfield alive, a fact that I wasn't sure how to take.

The service was just a few days later. It was held in a small church in the Mission. Despite the short notice, the place was overflowing with people: colleagues, family, classmates, even executives and Silicon Valley company founders who he'd met along the way. There were a handful of limos parked in the church's parking lot. Whitfield had never married, but that had not prevented him from casting a wide social net. Gosling didn't attend, but he sent an enormous bouquet of flowers, a thoughtful gesture that I was sure Priya had played a role in orchestrating. I sat in the last pew, dry-eyed and numb.

Whitfield's body was cremated, and after the service a small group of people – family and close friends – went to Muir Woods to disperse the ashes. I wasn't invited, which was fine and understandable.

To get to the church I'd ordered a Lyft car service, but I decided to walk back home, or, more accurately, to Gosling's home. It was a long way. I had tucked a joint into a pocket. I'd planned to smoke it during the walk – a sort of homage to my departed friend. I did smoke it, but regretted doing so almost immediately. The buzz at first heightened my feeling of loss, and then distorted it, didn't allow me to properly work through my emotions.

I spent the remainder of the day holed up in the mansion on Broadway. Magnus Carlsen must have recognized my dour mood (animals do have a sixth sense), because he spent the entire day nearby, occasionally rubbing his head against my arm, offering solace.

42

Roma was itching for trouble, a cathartic release. He'd gotten wind of a newly created community, a lawless city populated with thugs and rogue gamers bent on killing and mayhem. After popping open a text window and writing the code for an Indiana Jones-style change of clothes – leather jacket, fedora, and whip – he decided to take a walk along one of the city's alleys.

It was dark. Roma approached what from the outside appeared to be a bawdy bar. The building rocked, the sound of raised voices drifted through the walls. Roma lifted the collar on his jacket and entered the front door.

Once inside he had a prickly feeling, like every set of eyes in the joint had turned toward him. From the ceiling hung two cages, each cage was occupied with a naked woman whose body was so perfect it would put Aphrodite to shame. From the neck down both of the ladies were as smooth and hairless as a Georgia peach. The women looked at Roma, delivered lusty smiles. And then one of them yelled, "Kill that asshole!"

Roma spun just in time to see an over-sized brute try to cut his head off with a four-foot blade. Roma grabbed the brute's arm in mid-swing, yanked it clean off at the shoulder, and then using both hands twisted his attacker's head until his neck snapped. The dead man's body hit the ground with a satisfying thud.

Seizing on Roma's preoccupation with the first assailant, three men jumped him. One grabbed him by the legs while the second wrapped an arm around Roma's neck and proceeded to choke him. The third readied his fist to punch Roma square in the solar plexus. Roma kneed the puncher in the balls and then delivered a death punch between the eyes. He pried one man off his neck, the other off his leg, and smashed their heads together, shattering their skulls.

"Who's next?" Roma asked. He glanced around the room and took in maybe half a dozen other gamers. They moved toward Roma, hesitated, and then sunk into the woodwork.

"Come on, you pussies," shrieked one of the naked, caged women. "You're not going to just let this guy get away!"

Roma did an audit of the crowd. He spied a man with a bloodthirsty look on his face. The man fingered the handle of his sword, but he seemed to think better of it and let his hand fall harmlessly to his side.

"Smart choice," Roma said, and as he spoke he felt a whoosh of air rush past his ear. A split second later he heard the sound of a knife lodging itself in the wall behind him. By the trajectory of the blade's flight it was clear that it had been thrown by one of the two naked women, although where she'd stored the weapon was a complete mystery. Roma yanked the knife out of the wall threw it back at his attacker, hitting her directly where her third eye would have resided.

Roma looked up at the other woman, gave her a wave, and said, *"Ciao bella."* He then disappeared, leaving those who remained in the room to wonder what had hit them.

≈≈≈

"Back to open the hole again, I see," said the big-eyed Halfling.

Roma studied the odd little guy and was hit again with the same vexing itch that he'd felt before.

"That's right."

"What's with the new outfit?"

Roma looked down at his clothes and realized he hadn't bothered to change back to his standard outfit. "I just felt like a change."

Then Roma got down to work.

Even though it had been a while since he'd last worked on the hole, things went more quickly than before. Lessons learned had made the coding easier. Roma stopped, pulled out his caliper, and measured the progress. The hole was eight-tenths of a millimeter larger than before. Clearly, a recognizable pattern had emerged, one that perhaps should have been obvious sooner. Roma started to calculate how long until the hole would be wide enough for him to squeeze through, if what appeared to be happening continued. He didn't come to a clear resolution because the Halfling cut into his thoughts.

"Getting so close!" The Halfling exclaimed, gleefully. Then he made that odd sound again: "*Hmmmaaa ... hmmmaaa ... hmmmaaa ...*"

Roma nodded.

"Any luck finding that Troll?" The Halfling looked down as he asked, rubbed the dirt with his toe, as if giving the impression that he was inquiring in an off-hand way. But the show came off as too forced. It was clear to Roma that the Halfling did know more about the Troll than he was letting on.

"No," Roma said, "I've actually decided to stop looking for him." Not really true, but Roma wanted to throw the lying little guy a curveball.

"What?" The Halfling's head lifted, quickly. A butterfly descended into his mop of hair and stayed there, partially buried.

"Why bother?" Roma said. "I have no idea how to find him. And besides, he's the one who contacted me. I think it's on him to get in touch with me again."

The butterfly shifted its position, burrowed a little deeper into the Halfling's hair. The Halfling's eyes widened.

"But I thought you were curious about him?"

Roma was still holding the caliper in his hand and slid it back into his pocket. "I am, but what can I do?"

"And your girlfriend, Jett, you're not looking for her either?"

"No. Not really. I think it's time to move on." Then Roma threw this out there: "Unless I can find someone to help me, I think I've hit a dead end."

The Halfling stayed quiet.

"I had another good friend who just disappeared," Roma said. "A really good friend. My best friend. He sent me a note and asked me to jump on a plane and join him, but when I did I couldn't find him."

The Halfling looked deflated, like someone had stolen his lunch money.

Roma continued. "So I think I'm going to take a break, at least for now. Clear my head."

It looked like the little guy wanted to say something, but he was biting his lower lip, literally, so it couldn't move.

43

The day after Whitfield's funeral it poured.

The rain fell in relentless sheets – ponderous and inspiring – the type of rain that I've found is unique to Northern California; rain that marches down from Alaska, gathers steam from the Pacific, barrels onshore, and fuels the growth of redwood trees. But it wasn't winter, it was only October. It was too early for any type of rain in California, let alone a fierce winter-like storm. Yet a storm had come just the same.

Priya had told me she didn't believe in omens, so she wouldn't have bestowed any special meaning on the storm. It had come, it was there, and so be it. But I wasn't so sure. Maybe there are things in this world that can't be explained by simply relying on science? Who knows? Whatever its cause, the weather did reflect my mood. Without getting too maudlin or dramatic, my soul felt stormy. The storm was so fierce that it wasn't possible to see the view outside Gosling's window. It was frankly impossible to see beyond the edge of the patio.

So I drank a lot of coffee and surfed the 'Net on my iPad. I wasn't looking for anything, just roaming. I could hear the rain pelting the roof. I ended up on a page of literary quotes. How did I get there? I'm not sure. Click one link, another, another, and pretty soon you don't know where you've landed. On the page was a quote by Herman Melville, a bit of text from *Moby Dick* that caught my eye. It read:

"Whenever I find myself growing grim about the

mouth; whenever it is a damp, drizzly November in my soul; whenever I find myself involuntarily pausing before coffin warehouses, and bringing up the rear of every funeral I meet; and especially whenever my hypos get such an upper hand of me, that it requires a strong moral principle to prevent me from deliberately stepping into the street, and methodically knocking people's hats off - then, I account it high time to get to sea as soon as I can."

There was no attribution, although I assumed it was said by Ishmael. But what a quote! And boy, did it capture my mood. I felt like knocking off some hats, at least metaphorically. Venturing to the sea, however, was out of the question, for a variety of reasons, but mainly because I had absolutely zero interest. But I needed to get out, go for a walk, clear my head. Although it was still raining cats and dogs I didn't care. I found a parka and a large umbrella in Gosling's closet and headed out the front door.

I went for a really long walk, one that took me from Gosling's house on Pacific Heights all the way to Geary Street, just a block south of Union Square. Because of the heavy rain, I had the sidewalks mostly to myself. I was still shaken up by Whitfield's death and as a result I was lost in my thoughts.

Because I was so preoccupied, I didn't at first hear someone calling out to me. But then the voice grew louder, "Hey!"

I turned my head toward the street and saw a long black limousine. The back window was down and Roderick Jaynes was smiling at me. The sky darkened, and I felt touched by a finger of dread.

"Kind of an ugly day to be outside isn't it?" he asked.

At that moment his accent sounded more English than Midwestern, although it was still hard to pin down. Either way, it had a malevolent quality. Was this encounter by chance, or was Jaynes following me? It was impossible to know. I continued walking. The limo moved along the road, kept pace. "Are you about to offer me another brownie?" I asked out of the side of my mouth.

"You're still hung up on that?"

"I was passed out on the street. A crazy homeless man stole my shoe and phone." Not to mention the fact that I'd peed all over myself, I thought.

"Things happen in business."

I took a deep breath. "Business? Really? Drugging someone doesn't strike me as standard business protocol."

He snorted. "Don't be melodramatic. Let's put it behind us, okay?"

I didn't say anything.

"Look," said Jaynes, "Let me make it up to you. Let's talk."

"Cut the shit," I said, and glared at him. "Why would I want to talk to you?" I'd arrived at the end of the block. The light was red. I considered running away, but before I could Jaynes cut in.

"You want to talk to me because I have some additional information on the Troll. Now would that interest you?"

I forced a shrug. But certainly, I was interested.

"Come on. Ten minutes. That's all I need. Hop in."

"You're crazy. There's no way I'm getting inside that car." If we were to talk it had to be on neutral ground, and besides, I feared that the awful B.O. would still be lodged inside.

"Okay. Let me buy you a cup of coffee." He opened the back door and a whoosh of rancid air escaped. It smelled like death. Jaynes stepped out and onto the curb. The rain pelted his head. I caught a glimpse of one of his brutish goons inside the car. Jaynes led the way into a crowded deli and I followed. I know what you're thinking: I was nuts. Most people would have bolted, even if he did have more information on the Troll. The guy had drugged me and dumped me in Chinatown. But my curiosity overwhelmed any caution I should have felt.

We found a booth in the corner, lodged in between a couple of young marrieds and some businessmen in suits. Jaynes ordered for us: bagels and lox and capers and onions and cream cheese. We also each got a coffee, which was God awful, but did succeed in warming me up.

"You've dropped off the map," Jaynes said. His eyes were dark, almost black. "Where you've been keeping yourself?"

There was zero chance I was going to respond. Although his question led me to believe that our encounter had been happenstance. Life works out that way sometimes.

"Have it your way." Jaynes took a sip of his coffee, which he drank black. I added some cream and then followed suit. It tasted like old leather. Out of habit, I checked my phone for messages, but there were none.

"So I've had some research done," Jaynes said, "and it turns out you weren't kidding about the Troll playing high school basketball. He really did."

I didn't have anything to add.

"And he surfed, too. Did you know that?"

I shrugged.

"And he was really into Quantum Mechanics."

So far it was mostly information that I'd learned from Gosling. And by the look on Jaynes' face I gathered that he knew that. He hesitated for a moment, dramatically lifted an eyebrow as if he understood he was about to tell me something interesting.

"Did you know that Einstein didn't believe that Quantum Mechanics could be real, despite the evidence?"

"That's news to me." Honestly, I had almost no understanding of what Quantum Mechanics were.

"It was news to me as well. He used to say, 'God does not play dice.' That's because Quantum Mechanics don't deal in direct cause and effect. Two things can be true simultaneously, and how it ultimately plays out depends on how something is measured or how it is perceived."

"Fascinating. Do you have a point?"

"It is. It is fascinating. Stick with me here. So what if someone built a quantum computer?" He let the question hover in the air, and then continued. "Because of its simultaneous capabilities, it would likely vastly outperform a traditional computer, at least at certain tasks. As you know, computers today use bits – 0s or 1s. Binary code. And everything – every program, every line of code – is ultimately broken down, translated into that binary code."

He was right, I did know that.

"Well," he went on, "a quantum computer would do things differently. It would use quantum bits, or qubits, which can be both a zero or a one simultaneously."

I stopped him. "Excuse me?"

The food arrived, although neither one of us touched it. But the waiter freshened up our coffee and we drank it. "That's right," Jaynes continued, "it can be both at the same time. So you can see how that could speed up performance."

I could see the potential, I told him.

"From what I've read, it's believed that a quantum computer could be particularly useful at breaking through encryption barriers, making it much easier for organizations to read secret information that's posted online. And *everything* these days is posted online. But that's just one potential application. People aren't really even sure what these computers could do, how much the performance could improve. But it holds the potential to dramatically change the computing landscape. It would allow us to take a giant step forward."

Jaynes lathered half a bagel with cream cheese, added lox and the other ingredients. He took an enormous bite. A glob of cream cheese clung to his upper lip and he spoke with his mouth full of food. "Are you finding this interesting? Should I continue?"

I nodded.

"I'm sorry, I didn't hear you."

"Yeah, go on," I said.

He took another bite and then wiped his lip with a paper napkin. "Now here's the thing – these quantum computers are in the infancy stage. I'm talking strictly theoretical. Or at least that's what everyone thought."

"But you think the Troll has built one?"

"Bingo." He pointed at me with his index finger and then touched the tip of his nose.

I asked him how he'd come to that conclusion.

He grinned. "I need to keep my little secrets. But let's just say I have my means."

I'd heard that line before.

"And I'll be honest with you," said Jaynes, "I'm not completely clear what the Troll has come up with. I just have bits and pieces at this point. I've never even met the Troll, never seen a picture of him. Yet I find myself preoccupied with what he's up to. Why do you think that is?"

I had no idea.

"Really, I can't be certain myself. But let's call it intuition based on years of experience. The first time I learned about the Troll I was hit with a belief that I needed to keep an eye on him, in whatever way was possible. I knew that the man I represent would expect that of me. So I made it a top priority. I've been in this racket long enough that I've learned to follow my gut."

Once again, I had nothing to add, so I drank some

coffee, just to keep myself occupied.

Jaynes kept going. "But what's really puzzling is how do you fit into the equation? The Troll contacted you, so there's got to be some reason he thinks you'd be useful. Does anything come to mind?"

I thought about it. I wasn't sure. The Troll and his motivations were mysteries to me.

But as I sat in the coffee shop, I could see the pieces moving into their proper positions, like a well-orchestrated chess game. There was the Troll, the Halfling, and now a quantum computer. You could throw Nika into the mix. Move one here, shift another one there, and maybe back this one up two squares. But there were some pieces missing, gaps in the strategy. Still, it wasn't as hazy as before, it was starting to take shape.

"Nothing comes to mind," I lied. I looked Jaynes square in the eye, feigned earnestness.

Jaynes nodded in a way that seemed to indicate he didn't really believe me. He took another bite of his bagel, a slightly smaller one this time, and then washed it down it some coffee. He pulled a business card out of the breast pocket of his shirt and handed it to me. His hand brushed against mine. His fingers were icy, frigid.

"Regardless, the man I represent has instructed me to make you an offer."

Jaynes pulled a pen and a packet of Post-it notes out of the inside pocket of his jacket. He put them down on the Formica tabletop and scribbled something. He pulled off the top piece of paper and handed it to me. I read it. There was a seven-figure number written on the note.

"That would be your signing bonus. You'd be on retainer, and would report direct to me. When we got more information on what the Troll is up to you'd be put to work."

I studied the note and then looked at Jaynes. He

handed me his business card.

"Take a few days and think about the offer. Then call me," he said.

I told him I would, although there was zero chance of that happening. He'd always be an asshole in my book. No amount of money would change that. The bill arrived and he grabbed it. "You never even touched your food," he said.

When we stepped outside, the rain had stopped but the sky was still black. Rivers of water rushed down the streets, flooded into the sewers. I tucked my umbrella under my arm.

"Let me give you a ride home," Jaynes offered, as we stood under the awning.

I told him I'd rather get home on my own.

"Suit yourself." He walked slowly to his black limo, which was now double parked, climbed into the backseat. Once inside and the door closed, he lowered his window and yelled to me, "Call me if you hear from the Troll. I'll make it worth your while." The window went up. I couldn't see through the black tint. The car plodded down the street. I crumpled up the Post-it and Jaynes' business card and deposited them in the nearest garbage can.

≈≈≈

I walked over to Market Street, to the dilapidated section where homeless men play chess. Because of poor weather there were only three men out there, their chessboards setup on rickety folding tables, plastic chairs on either side.

"Wanna play?" I asked one of the men, who by the look of him I guessed was the strongest player.

"Five minutes, three dollars each game to the winner," he said, in a thick Russian accent. He wore a wool trench coat and a felt hat.

We played four games and I won every one. He opted

for bizarre and unorthodox openings, moves designed to confuse the average fish, but they were unsound and I easily skated past any trouble, slowly accumulating advantages until I squeezed the life out of him. We played one more game, but by then he was rattled and lost quickly.

"Go away," he said, his voice an angry growl. "You're too good."

He dug a fistful of crumbled bills out of his coat pocket and tried to hand them to me, but I told him to keep them.

I walked up Powell Street and hailed a cab in front of the St. Francis hotel. I asked the driver to take a circuitous route back to Gosling's house, just to make sure we weren't being followed.

44

Back at Gosling's house I took a shower. Night had settled in so when I finished I slipped into pajama bottoms and a T-shirt. I went online and checked my bank account and saw that another paycheck from Gosling had been deposited. It was a good deal of coin for basically doing nothing.

Hungry, I made a simple meat sauce and boiled up some pasta. I ate it, using a piece of sour dough bread to help mop up the plate. Looking out the westward windows, it had started to rain again, a gentle mist.

After feeding Magnus, I grabbed a joint and took my customary spot on the sofa. I planned to smoke it and then go online to read about quantum computers when I heard my cell phone ring. I couldn't locate it at first, but eventually found it inside the pocket of the parka I'd worn that day. I answered it just before it would have rolled into voicemail. Priya was on the other end.

"Hi. Is this a good time?" she asked.

It was fine, I told her.

"I just wanted to call and let you know I was sorry to hear about the death of your friend, Whitfield."

"Thank you. I appreciate that. And I saw the flowers you sent – that was thoughtful."

"He was the one who contacted Mr. Gosling on your behalf. Were you close?"

"We'd only known each other a short time, but yes, we were close. Have you ever met someone and almost immediately felt a connection to them, like you were meant to be friends?"

"I have, but it's rare."

"It is rare. Anyway, that's the way it was with Whitfield and me."

"Well again, I'm really sorry." There was a short pause and then she said, "I also called because I wanted to make sure that your paychecks are going through."

She was a mind reader, that Priya. "I actually just checked my account. Yeah, it's all good."

"Great. And thank you for helping out."

"It's been easy." Shifting gears, I asked, "So how's school?"

"Great, it's really great, actually. I'm getting close to graduating."

"That would be quite an accomplishment. I never even graduated from college."

"Yes, I know that."

"You do?"

"Whenever Mr. Gosling has an appointment – like the one he had with you – it's my responsibility to put together a briefing book with details about that person. So I know quite a bit about you."

I wasn't sure how to take that. "What else do you know?"

"I know that you went to Stanford. I know you started a company, but it didn't take off. I know you worked at Centre Terrain, but that's obvious. I know you're considered a brilliant programmer."

"You should make it that I *was* considered a decent programmer. I don't remember the last time I wrote a line of code, unless it was somehow tied to Centre Terrain."

"I wouldn't let that bother you. A lot of people go through fallow periods in their careers. This is just yours. You'll bounce back stronger."

"You think so?"

"Absolutely. I think those down periods can be really beneficial, especially after the experience of running a start-up. People need to recharge their batteries."

Was that all I was doing – recharging my batteries? With Italy and my newly established weed habit, Center Terrain and especially the cake job house sitting for Gosling, I felt like I'd firmly locked myself into "being" mode. My doer days were behind me.

I mumbled something incoherent.

"Maybe you just need to be inspired – find some new seeds to plant."

"You really think so?"

"Yes. We can never escape who we truly are, and you're a programmer."

We stayed on the phone for another half hour, talked about the unseasonal rain and other mundane topics. When we hung up I fingered the joint I'd rolled, smoked it. I went to the fridge and pulled out a beer. I flipped on the TV and watched reruns of *Seinfeld* and *Friends* until I fell asleep on the sofa.

45

That night I dreamed about Whitfield. He was dressed in a white tuxedo with tails and a white bowtie. He stood alone in a dark room.

"Are you here to say goodbye?" I asked.

"No. I'm here to play chess."

Just like that a marble chessboard materialized in front of us. The squares were black and white, the pieces carved with expert care. Two chairs appeared as well and Whitfield and I sat, assumed the standard positions, prepared for battle.

"Smoke?" I asked.

"No. Not here." His eyes studied the board and then rose up to look at me. "You know what I like about chess?" he asked.

I shrugged.

"Nothing is hidden. There are no tricks, no sleight of hand. It's all right there, just laid out before you. No luck either. You can't complain about the sun being in your eyes or bad officiating or your partner missing an easy shot. It's just you and the opponent, let the best man win."

"It's poetic, in its own way."

He nodded. "Still, people can't see the truth."

"It's not easy to see. It's complex."

"It is. But you gotta try. You gotta put in the effort."

"Are we still talking about chess?"

Whitfield smiled. "What else is there?"

We started to play. Days passed and then weeks. We pushed pieces across the board for centuries, eons. Time merged with space, the movement of the pieces assumed their own life until their movements morphed into the only reality. We played at lightning speed, striving to execute every possible move, or failing that, willing to accept the disintegration of the universe – whichever came first.

46

The sun had returned and as a result of all the rain the sky was exceptionally clear and bright. I'd never seen a bluer sky than those in San Francisco.

Magnus Carlsen had slept on the sofa as well. Together we worked our way to the kitchen where we each ate a hearty breakfast.

I know what I need to do, I thought, between bites of toast.

I refilled my coffee cup and then got stoned, I mean really, really high. I was still somewhat buzzed from the previous night and felt encased with a lulling contentment, a kind of peaceful and dreamy detachment. The other result was that I became hungry – famished – despite the fact that I had almost literally just polished off a rather large breakfast. So I rummaged in the kitchen, devoured a banana as I whipped up two scrambled eggs and toast. In less than an hour's time I ate two entire meals.

Once my hunger was satiated, I decided to just explore the house. Although Priya, on that first day I'd arrived, had given me a complete tour, I hadn't spent time in more than a handful of rooms. I had no specific destination in mind, nothing I particularly wanted to see. I was just killing time.

Eventually I ended up in the greenhouse. It was bright and spacious, a good deal larger than my entire apartment. The air was dewy and smelled heavenly. I could hear water running. I inhaled the moist air, lifted my face upward to let the sun shine on it, walked aimlessly down one of the paths. I didn't get far until my progress was blocked by a woman who was kneeling on the ground and tending the plants. Her presence caused me to wonder again why Gosling had deemed it necessary for me to look after his home. From the little I'd seen there was a small army of workers who made sure everything was taken care of. But you and I can't really understand how the minds of the filthy rich work, no more than an ant can appreciate the lives that we lead.

At first the woman didn't notice me. Her hands were covered with dark, rich-looking soil, and she was busy re-planting an orchid. She was old, gray haired, and for some reason she reminded me of an aunt on my mother's side who died when I was eight. The aunt was a sweet old lady who used to bake me brownies and sneak candy so that my health-conscious mother wouldn't be aware. A memory flashed of her dropping a lollipop into my coat pocket, which caused me to laugh, drawing the attention of the woman on the ground. She stopped planting the orchid and turned her gaze toward me.

The woman said something in a language that I didn't understand, and then shot me a look of reproach. She sniffed, her nose moving like a curious rabbit, and I was hit with a paranoid feeling that she could smell the pungent aroma of sinsemilla. She spoke again, and although I still couldn't understand her it was clear by her expression that she wanted me to leave.

I returned to the kitchen.

There I was somewhat embarrassed to find two more women cleaning up. One of them was scrubbing the dishes that I'd left on the counter while the other was opening a can of sardines for Magnus while he waited patiently on the ground. Clearly it was cleaning day.

"Beautiful cat," said the woman with the sardines.

I told her thank you.

"What's his name?"

"Magnus Carlsen."

She frowned. "That's an unusual name for a cat."

I suppose, I said.

An expression crossed her face that seemed indicate that she had reconsidered her comment, and she said, "I know that name. He's a famous chess player, right?"

I told her she was right.

"He's a prodigy, a genius. My son, he told me about Magnus Carlsen. My son, he's a chess player." She smirked. "Of course, the best players are all computers now."

"True," I conceded, bitterly.

I know what I need to do, I thought again. But I wasn't ready to do it, not just yet.

We gaped at each other for a bit and I decided that I wanted some privacy, so I went to the theater and locked the door behind me. In Gosling's video library, I found a copy of *The Departed*. After loading it up, I settled into the front row and got ready to watch Jack and Leonardo and the rest of the boys do their thing. I wished I had a big bag of popcorn.

≈≈≈

When the movie ended, I gathered my laptop and augmentation glasses and went to Gosling's office. I planned to log into Centre Terrain. I was about to slip on the glasses, but stopped myself and decided to get stoned again. I'd become a regular smoking fiend. But *The Departed* is a long movie, and while watching it my buzz had evaporated. I dug a half-finished joint out of my shirt pocket and lit it with a Bic lighter. The room filled with smoke, my head spun. I deposited the roach that remained into my pants pocket.

≈≈≈

The mushrooms had multiplied. A thick carpet of moss – newly installed – covered the ground. The air was heavy, swampy. Roma looked around for the Halfling, but he wasn't there. No worries. He'd arrive, he always did. And it didn't take long. Roma only had to wait a few minutes until the Halfling materialized, just formed in mid-air.

"Here to work on the hole," he said. "And this time it will go even faster. *Hmmmaaa...*"

Roma didn't respond. The Halfling looked at him, Roma returned his gaze. This went on for a bit until the Halfling said, "Are you going to get to work?"

Roma sized up the Halfling, let his eyes scan him from foot to head, before asking, "Captain – that's you, right?"

The question hung in the air, just lingered above them. After a couple of ticks of the clock the Halfling inched closer to Roma, sniffed. "Are you stoned?" he asked.

"Yes. It's a habit I picked up."

The Halfling shook his head disapprovingly. "It doesn't suit you."

Roma let that comment go.

"How'd you know it was me?" the Captain asked.

"I didn't, not at first, not consciously at least. But the truth snuck up on me until it was inescapable. And the Troll confirmed it, in his own cryptic way."

The Captain's head bobbed.

"So why keep it a secret?" Roma asked.

The Captain paused for a moment, considered his response. "Not everything can be explained, not rationally, not in a way that would make sense. I just felt like secrecy was the route to go. Can you understand that?"

No, Roma didn't understand, but he kept mum.

"Although, if you must have an explanation," the Captain continued, "it's safe to say that I was embarrassed. I'm not just another character in the game, I'm locked in here. I'm a fully digital being, maybe the first, a pioneer. *Hmmmaaa...*" he coughed, like there was something dead inside him that needed to escape.

"I gathered that," said Roma. "And that's why you weren't there when I arrived, when I flew back from Italy?"

"That's right. I'd intended to be, but then this happened." Using both hands the Captain let his fingers brush from his feet upwards.

"Are you dead?" Roma asked.

"Dead. No. But. I'm...I'm not living. Not in the way you may normally imagine life. But I am alive. I don't mean to be so enigmatic."

"What happened?"

A gigantic rabble of butterflies lifted from off the tops of the mushrooms. They filled the sky, blocked out the light, swayed rhythmically as if dancing to a lively, unheard tune. Roma and the Captain watched as the swarm slowly flew away until they were just a dark smudge in the distance.

Roma pulled his eyes from the butterflies and looked at the Captain. "So what happened?" Roma repeated.

"Okay, I'll tell you. But it might take a while. Let's sit." They found a large boulder and sat together.

47

"So you met the Troll," the Captain said.

"Uh-huh, I did, through my processor."

The Captain smiled, knowingly. "He has a flair for the dramatic, doesn't he? Let me guess – he dropped you in a bright yellow room, there was a word cloud and words like, 'Future' and 'Exponential' and 'Singularity' swirled around your head?"

'No, it wasn't like that." Roma described the scene: the darkness and the doors, the binary code and 3-D spheres.

The Captain snorted. "So he mixes up his little performances. I should have guessed."

"You met him in a similar way?"

"No, that came later. You need a neural processor for a show like that. I met the Troll in a bar."

"A bar?"

The Captain nodded his head. "That's right, a real hole in the wall, South of Market. I'd never been there before and I can't for the life of me tell you why I ended up in it that night. Do you believe in fate or the idea of a guiding hand?"

Roma shook his head. "Not really. Although I'm starting to believe there might be something to omens, even if they can be a little heavy handed at times."

The Captain shook his head. "I don't buy any of it. It's all just hocus-pocus bullshit. So why did I go to that particular bar on that particular day? Let's just call it happenstance. I happened to go into that bar and I happened to order a beer and the Troll happened to saddle

255

up on the adjacent stool. You could have knocked me over with a feather. Here's this guy – the Troll – all seven feet of him, sitting next to me in a bar. That day he sported a full beard, trimmed neatly, and I kid you not, a gray Armani suit. Can you imagine how much it must have cost to get that thing custom made? He was a freak, but damn, he looked sharp."

One lone butterfly remained. It was a tiny monarch. The butterfly rested on top of a purple mushroom. It leaned slightly toward the Captain, as if listening.

"You actually met the Troll?" Roma asked. "You're the first person I know who has, except me. The rest just learned about him through someone else, secondhand."

"Yeah, like I just told you, I met him. Anyway, at the bar, the Troll ordered a beer. His hand was so large the pint glass fit into his palm. He sat right next to me and besides the two of us and the bartender, you the place is empty. I did my best to ignore the Troll, but when I finished my beer he offered to buy me another. I sprang for the round after that and that's when we get to talking. So..."

The Captain trailed off. His eyes drifted upward. Roma waited a bit and then injected, "So you and the Troll are drinking beers..."

The Captain snapped to attention. "Sorry about that. I'm kind of losing myself. I'm still here, but more Halfling than Captain."

"How did you end up as a Halfling?" Roma asked again.

"I told you, we'll get to that later. Now where was I? Oh yeah, the Troll and I get to talking. Somehow the conversation steers toward Polpo and when it does I could see his ears perk up."

"'You worked for a start-up?' the Troll asked."

"'Launched it,' I told him. He asked me for specifics

and I provided them, detailed everything. He grilled me about every aspect of the company, but was particularly interested in all the programming work. So I spelled it out, outlined all the work that I'd done."

Roma raised an eyebrow. "All the work that *you'd* done?"

The Captain rolled his head in a circle, an awkward and uncomfortable looking move. "That's right, the work *I'd* done." He paused and looked Roma square in the eye. "In other words, I lied. Or at least stretched the truth to the point where it was no longer recognizable."

Roma shrugged. "Whatever. Go on."

"The Troll and I shut the bar down. We drank beer after beer, ate onion rings, and talked about Polpo. Near 2:00 a.m., the bartender flicked on the overhead lights. That's when the Troll told me he was working on a new project, something potentially big."

"And your eyes got wide."

The Captain smiled. "You know me. Yeah, I got interested, real interested. I sniffed something juicy. During that night, the Troll had mostly listened. Still, I could sense there was something about that cat – he had that certain quality. It was the same way with you, back at Stanford."

The Captain's eyes went upward again. "*Hmmmaaa...*" he said. Roma thought he was going to lose him. Then the Captain twisted his neck, cracked a couple of vertebrae, his eyes cleared.

"So I got him to agree to meet me again the next night," the Halfling continued, "at the same bar. Even then he wasn't completely forthcoming. But in time, over a few nights, I got him to open up."

"And he told you he was building a quantum computer?"

The Captain nodded. "Someone's been doing his

homework. Yeah, that's right. And it sounded revolutionary. But the thing is the Troll was strictly a hardware guy, or so he told me. He needed someone to write code and tie it all together."

"And that's where you came in. You convinced the Troll that you were the man for the job."

"Exactly. I volunteered to write a program, a prototype."

"What type of program?"

"Another gaming system, like Centre Terrain, only better. But really it would be more than just a simple game. From what the Troll told me, with his new hardware, the user experience would be mind-blowing, essentially a *real* world, a new world, a place where people could practically live full time. It would be like something out of science fiction."

The Captain paused for minute, caught his breath, and then spoke up. "But I was in over my head. That's when I sent you that email. I gather you got the note."

Roma nodded.

"I was hoping you could come out and help."

"I hopped on a plane the next day."

The Captain shrugged. "I waited too long. By then I'd already finished a working version of the program. It was crap, but the Troll didn't know that. He wanted to give it a test drive. So he installed a neural processor in my head, we hacked into Centre Terrain, built a special patch so my code could be installed, we added what I'd written, and off I went. At first..."

The Captain's eyes drifted upward again. His lids lowered. "*Hmmmaaa...*" he said.

Roma could see that the Captain was slipping away. Using both hands, he grabbed him by the shoulders and gently rocked him. "Are you in there?" he asked. "I have a few questions." The Captain's eyes cracked open. He looked subdued, like he'd lost a piece of himself. Something that should have lived there was gone.

"At first it worked okay," the Captain continued, eventually. "In fact, better than okay, I'd created something rather cool."

"Really?" Roma asked, incredulously.

The Captain scowled. "I know, you think I'm worthless, that I have no programming chops. Granted, I'm not the ace you are, but I've learned a trick or two over the years."

"Okay. Go on."

"But something went wrong. I can't explain it, not in a way that makes sense. But somehow I just got consumed *into* the program. I'm stuck here, and like I said, the part of me that's the Captain is slowly slipping away."

The sky darkened, an unseen light source dimmed. Roma felt a swell of melancholy rush over him.

"So what about the hole?" Roma asked. "Why are you so intent on having me open it?"

"The Troll is on the other side, at least that's what I think. And if you get through..." The Captain's eyes rolled upward again. He shook his head and jostled the pupils back into their rightful positions. "If you get through I'm hoping I can follow. I tried to open it myself, but I couldn't. It's beyond me. But you've seemed to figure it out, yes?"

Roma nodded. "Yes. You could say that. And it's getting bigger exponentially, right? That's something you recognize as well?"

"That's right."

The Captain's eyes – those big, sad eyes – opened wider. He looked around, but Roma couldn't tell if his mind registered what he saw. The Captain seemed to focus on something that wasn't there, something that wasn't visible to Roma.

"That's all for now," he whispered, "I need to be going."

Then, like the Cheshire Cat, he faded away until he was gone.

All that was left was an eerie silence, the removal of noise, like a book that's finished and closed shut.

48

I looked in a full-length mirror. My face was swollen, a gut stretched my shirt. All the weed and Bloody Marys had helped tack on the weight.

The roach in my pocket seemed to whisper, "So what's a few pounds? I still got some left in me. Let's have another go..."

I stripped, took in my naked reflection, was turned off by what I saw.

"Meow, meow, meow..." Magnus Carlsen was calling me, but when I scanned the room he was nowhere to be found.

I located a bathroom that I'd never used before and puked out the contents of my stomach. I didn't feel sick, but whatever lived inside was fighting to get out: a purging. Once all the food had escaped, I clung to the toilet bowl, pressed my face against the cold porcelain.

"Radios," said Whitefield, "they all took them apart, every one of them."

"You need me," said the Captain.

There are 10^{120} possible moves in a game of chess, and only 10^{75} atoms in the entire universe. Wrap you head around that. But here's the thing: you don't need to see all of the moves, just uncover the best next one. And then the one after that, followed by the one after that. I thought about the apparent simplicity of that and for a moment time grinded to a stop.

I ran the shower. The hot water warmed my shivering body.

I was stretched out on an operating table. A doctor looked down at me, smiled, held a tiny processor between his thumb and forefinger. "You'll be new and improved," he says. "Now close your eyes, you won't feel a thing."

Dried, dressed for bed, I made my way to the bedroom, but stopped, turned around, headed for Gosling's main room. Something told me I should sleep on the sofa. Through the window I could see the Golden Gate Bridge glowing in the distance. Draped on the sofa was a throw blanket that I used to cover my body.

"Meow!" Magnus appeared and took his customary spot near my feet. His little body was pressed against me, warming my toes.

I closed my eyes and fell into a dream.

I was on a beach. It was balmy. Waves crashed onto the shore. The Troll sat on a towel, jotting notes on a piece of paper. He looked my way, nodded. He stood, grabbed a surfboard that had been sticking upright in the sand. "Gotta catch some waves," he said, and walked slowly toward the ocean.

"I wanted to ask you some questions," I blurted out.

"Come with me." The Troll kept moving, picked up speed. I tried to keep pace, but my feet were stuck. Soon the sand rose up to my knees.

"But I don't have a surf board."

"I guess you're out of luck," the Troll said. His skin was bronzed by the sun. "But don't worry, I'll be back."

The sun dropped below the horizon. The beach and the ocean disappeared from view. Floating in the darkness I saw three shadowy figures. They drifted toward me, flickering in and out of focus. I squinted, tried to make out who they were, but couldn't. Then I recognized the figures: Roderick Jaynes, Gosling, and the Halfling.

Jaynes spoke first. "Call me if you hear from the Troll. I'll make it worth your while."

Gosling said only, "He's a freak."

The Halfling spoke last. "You could have knocked me over with a feather."

"You're repeating yourselves," I said, but they didn't listen.

A halo of light formed around the Halfling's head and I thought I could make out the Captain's face underneath. It was a like a scar, hidden from view. The light dimmed again and the scarred image of the Captain disappeared. The Halfling said, "*Hmmmaaa...*"

He broke off from the other two. I watched as he walked in circles, blinking in and out of view.

I heard a soft voice. "Let me tell you about the Troll." It was Nika.

49

"Let me tell you about the Troll," said Nika. I knew she wasn't part of the dream. But the dream did continue, more odd happenings occurred, I simply chose to push it into the back of my mind.

I turned my focus toward Nika, and as I did a new world formed around me. It was dark, of course, it's always dark. And there were pinpricks of light; stars far in the distance. I looked down at my arm and could see my tattoo.

"We're inside our processors," I said.

"That's right."

"It looks like we're in space."

She laughed. She looked good, sexy, but in a more refined way. She was dressed in all black, head to toe, black pants and shoes and a pullover top. Her hair was pulled back into a ponytail, and I could see the smooth side of her face where the ear should be.

"I know," she said. "It's a little clichéd. I built it, a simple program. What do you think?"

"It'll do."

"So are you confused?" she asked. She scrunched her eyebrows and her face was covered with an expression of thoughtful concern.

"Confused. Yeah. Puzzled. Disoriented – that too. Although in its own bizarre way things are starting to make sense. It is definitely one of the weirdest, most unbelievable series of events I've encountered. But I've chosen to believe what I've seen."

She nodded.

"Can I ask you a question?" I asked.

"Sure."

"The sex – was that just a ploy for you to get closer to the Troll?"

"No," she said, without a moment's hesitation.

It was a lie, I suspected, a white one, but one I appreciated.

"So what comes next?" I asked.

"Oh that's easy. You write the program for the new and improved Centre Terrain."

"I write the program..."

"That's right. I took the code that your friend, the Captain, had started and I built on it. That's where I've been. The Troll recruited me and now I'm recruiting you. I could only take it so far, you're the man to finish the job."

I felt my shoulders slump. "So that's what this all comes down to, creating a new game, a new product that we can sell?"

She smiled, radiated. "You're looking at this wrong. It's not just a program. If we can build this – if you can write the code – we'll take a huge step forward toward a better place. We'll be soldiers on the front lines of the revolution. Don't downplay it. Business, technological advances – they often drive big steps forward, steps that change the trajectory of mankind, put us on a higher plane."

A higher plane – that struck me as rather hyperbolic. But her enthusiasm was contagious. I perked up. Although everything still wasn't clear to me, not fully.

"The Troll has finished building a quantum computer," Nika said. "I've seen it. It will blow your mind. All that work he did, all those years of just thinking that you told me about in your dreams, when the Troll was toiling away in solitude in the dilapidated apartment building – it's all built to this moment."

"What? You mean the dreams you had," I said, confused.

"No, *your* dreams, the dreams you had when you were younger. The one's you told me about that night at my apartment. You don't remember?"

The space around me seemed to twist. I felt dizzy, liquid. I reached to grab something to hold onto, to steady myself, but there was nothing there, just emptiness. The urge to vomit rose up from the depths of my stomach until I could taste it in my mouth. I pushed it back down.

"Who, or what, exactly, is the Troll?" I finally forced out.

"Who is he?" she said. "Is he a person, like you and me? I don't know. I didn't ask. He's obviously different, perhaps the result of radical evolution, although he's not necessarily better. But he does have an advanced understanding of certain things. Some of this understanding comes innately while the rest was cultivated through years of hard work. And he can help lead the way to the future, maybe even help get us there a little faster."

"What type of future?"

"That's still to be determined. That's for you to help decide," she answered, cryptically. "This project, the new Centre Terrain, that's just a stepping stone. You have to start somewhere."

She licked her lips with the tip of her tongue. "He sees special qualities in you."

"Me?"

"Isn't it obvious? You're clearly the best person to write the code to run on his new computer. Think about it – who knows Centre Terrain better than you do?"

I thought about it. No one did. The nauseated sensation eased a bit – a reprieve.

"Not even the original designers know all its ins and outs, what works and what doesn't, all its flaws," Nika said. "No one knows it like you do. No one. At first, the Troll would have been satisfied with just a radically improved game, a game where people could spend more time than they do in the real world. But since he's met the Captain he wants something more." She paused, built up the suspense. "He wants the audience measurement technology that you developed at Polpo, or at least a variant of it, incorporated into the game. So not only will we create a new world, but we'll be able to monitor every element of what the players in that world are doing, what their interests are, what drives them."

She paused again, floated slowly toward me.

"Can you see the opportunity?"

I nodded, but didn't say a word.

"Good. Then you need to get busy. I'll deliver the code that we've created and you can build on it. Well, I guess that's goodbye for now."

She turned, as if to leave, but then looked back.

"I'm glad we'll be working together."

50

Dawn broke and I was in a chipper mood. My head was clear, my thinking razor sharp. Magnus grumbled a bit, but after I'd looked after his needs he returned to his placid self. I ate breakfast, but no Bloody Marys, no weed. The desire to catch a buzz had completely dissipated. I'd turned the page.

I went online and in a few minutes found an assortment of articles about quantum computers. Words and phrases like: "Holy grail of physics" and "qubits" and "unreliable" and "orders of magnitude more powerful than today's supercomputers" and "still purely theoretical" jumped off the page. Teams of engineers had been formed around the world to crack the quantum computing nut, but none had succeeded. Yet, if I was to believe Nika – and I did believe her – the Troll had done it all on his own. Sometimes a single genius can succeed where a multitude of others cannot.

I dressed in jeans and a hoodie, the uniform of the programmer. I ate a banana and filled a large plastic cup with water. Returning to my Mac, I logged into my email and found a message from Nika containing the program she'd promised. It was very large and she'd sent it as a .zip file. It took over an hour to download. Once it finished, I immediately opened the file and read through the work that Nika and the Captain had started.

It was good.

No, it was damn good. At least it seemed that way at first blush. But as I dug deeper I uncovered areas for improvement. When the onion was peeled even further I found outright errors. Shit. It was all crap. Worthless! Everything would need to be reexamined, redone. I went through the program line by line, that's the only way. Time inched along until its gears stopped completely. Nothing existed except the task at hand. I entered a blissful, Zen-like trance. I was Zen. My eyes saw everything.

When I finally stopped for the day it was dark. I'd been working for hours without break. My spirit felt great, and I was ecstatic about what I'd accomplished. In just one day I'd written a program that was ready to take to the Troll.

≈≈≈

Not so fast.

The next day I realized that everything I'd done the previous day was wrong. Well, not *everything*, some of the underlying concepts might still pass muster, but the nitty-gritty code wouldn't fly. For starters, I'd written a program designed for a standard computer; it just wouldn't work for a quantum computer. I needed to write something for qubits, not binary code. But I didn't know where to begin.

I decided to go back to school, in a manner of speaking.

I went to Amazon and after reading a few reviews I downloaded what appeared to be the two best books on quantum programming. Over the next few days I read both books three times. I burrowed deep into the Internet and found a very compelling, exceedingly technical white paper on quantum programming. It was written by a German engineer with an unpronounceable name. Over the next few weeks I read and reread that white paper, cradled it to my mind, until I was sure I understood the concepts better than the author himself.

I was on my way.

The work on the new and improved, quantum-based Centre Terrain went slowly at first, but each day got a little better. My head started to piece together the puzzle, to untie the knots, to find the right series of moves. I maniacally wrote and rewrote the code, polished it with lapidary care. During this period, I stopped drinking alcohol altogether. I quit smoking pot entirely. I drank copious amounts of water, ate fruit and pasta. My mind was still. Each day, I started work early and ended late. And I entered a state of self-imposed isolation. My iPhone was turned off and I stuck it in the drawer of my bedside table. I only checked my email and text messages once a day, right before I climbed into bed. When the maids and other workers arrived at Gosling's house I hid in the office, locked the door. Magnus Carlsen was practically my only companion, and even those exchanges were kept to a minimum.

≈≈≈

But I didn't remain completely isolated. On three separate occasions I logged into Centre Terrain and Roma showed the Captain the progress that had been made. Each time the Captain seemed a little less *there*, like he could slip away permanently at any moment. He couldn't even speak, at least not understandably. The only sound he uttered was that one strange word: *Hmmmaaa* ...What remained of the Captain would soon be gone forever, and although this was a tragic fact, there was nothing either of us could do about it. Still, the Captain studied the scrolling code. To Roma, it seemed that he registered that real progress was being made. And he approved.

On a few occasions I was also contacted by Nika, through my processor, while I was asleep. The first time we discussed the progress that I'd made and she seemed awestruck.

"It sounds *amazing*," she said.

We made a pact that when I'd finished the work she'd

contact me and together we'd present it to the Troll.

Once, as I neared the finish line, she tried to contact me, but I was in the midst of a dream I didn't want to leave and I instinctually blocked her attempts to communicate. Until that moment I didn't know that I had that control. It was a discovery – a nugget of information – that I filed away for later.

≈≈≈

Days passed. Then I made a real breakthrough. I had a framework done. The work had gone fast, remarkably so considering I was doing something – writing code for a quantum computer – that no one had done before. I was plowing virgin snow. There was still work ahead, but I felt good.

To celebrate, I booked an appointment with the same tattoo artist I'd gone to before. I wanted an image of my name in qubits inked onto my other forearm.

"What's this," the artist asked, when he looked at the design I'd handed him.

"It's a little hard to explain."

"Whatever," he said, with a shake of his head.

≈≈≈

And then one afternoon it happened.

A few months after that first visit from the Troll I finished writing the code. Not *finished*, finished, it would need more work; a team of programmers to help complete, to polish it and shine it. But it was solid. I'd completed an alpha version of the program.

Damn: it sung.

It was ready to bring to the Troll.

51

To get to the Troll I needed to return to Centre Terrain and open the portal. It would take some doing, but it shouldn't eat up too much time. With each successive try the coding had gotten easier – I'd learned that.

The day after I'd finished writing the alpha version of the program I planned to login to Centre Terrain and go present the program to the Troll. But first I was hungry. So I ate a sandwich while sitting on a sofa in Gosling's great room. Two bites in, I heard a knock on the front door. I opened it up and was confronted by Priya. I hadn't seen her in weeks.

"You look good," she said. "Healthy. Can I come in?"

Of course, I told her.

She sat down on a wingchair and gazed out the westerly windows. It was white and foggy outside. Priya looked serious, like something was on her mind.

Something was.

"So," she said, "I have some bad news. At least I think it's bad."

"Oh yeah, what is it?"

"Mr. Gosling has asked that you leave his house. Nothing personal, but the housesitting has run its course."

Easy come, easy go, but it was okay by me. The timing somehow seemed appropriate.

"That's fine. When should I leave?"

"No hurry. Take a few days. We'll make sure you get a severance check. And we can send a car over to help transport your stuff. You still have you apartment on Nob

Hill, right?"

I told her that I did.

"Well that's settled." She opened the little purse she was carrying and pulled out a rectangular piece of paper. "Now for some good news." Priya stood, walked to where I was seated, handed me the paper.

I examined it. It was a check. The amount was for one hundred thousand dollars.

"What's this for?" I asked. She'd returned to her seat, crossed one leg over the other.

"It's to start your new company."

I looked down again at the check, back up at Priya.

"What company?"

"The new Centre Terrain, of course." A little smile started to dance across her face, which she quickly worked to conceal.

It took me a moment to register what was happening. Once I did I asked, "So you know about that?"

"Uh-huh."

"What do you know?"

"Everything."

"Everything?"

"Yes, everything."

"But how?"

She just shrugged. There was a lot of detail in that shrug, but a lot left out as well.

"I take it that Gosling wants to invest?" I asked.

"No. Not Mr. Gosling. Look at the check again."

I did as instructed. In the bottom right-hand corner, in the spot where the signature goes, Priya had scribbled her name.

"So you want to be an angel investor?" I asked.

She nodded. "That's right." Magnus took that moment to jump up on her lap. She softly rubbed the spot between his ears, without taking her eyes off me.

"And you have the kind of money?"

"I'm a good saver," she said. She took a small breath and then continued. "We'll work up a contract later. I left who the check is made out to blank. I figured you and the Troll can dream up a company name, hopefully something catchier than Centre Terrain. I've already started on a business plan, and even identified a few potential big-name investors. You have a series of meetings scheduled next week, by the way. I'm going to hire an admin, and she – or he – will organize your calendar. We're going to be busy."

She shifted her eyes and looked out the window again. I didn't follow her line of vision, but I like to believe that she was watching a white crane fly by, one of those crazy omens.

"We're meant to do this," she said, her eyes still glued to whatever she saw outside. "Together."

I started to laugh, a deep belly laugh, one that shook my whole body, brought fat tears to my eyes.

"Okay," I said. It was all I could manage. Using my thumb I wiped the moisture from my lids.

So I was back in the start-up game. There was just one thing left to do.

52

Roma opened a pop-up window and started to code. He hadn't bothered to use the caliper and measure the hole in the program. Roma had, however, looked for the Halfling, but he never found him. He waited a half hour before starting, but the Halfling never appeared. And he never would, not ever again. He was gone. Roma felt that.

Before he got to work, Roma could feel Nika trying to contact him through his processor. But he blocked her efforts. He effectively put up a firewall that she could not get through.

Nika wouldn't be going with him to see the Troll. She wasn't needed. Roma was sure that if the roles had been reversed she'd have done the same thing. If she could have written the program then she would have written the program and left him high and dry.

It's all business, he thought.

The mushrooms were still there, more of them, a lot more, and the butterflies as well. There were so many butterflies that the air hummed with the noise of their little flapping wings. A dozen of them rested on Roma's back as he worked to open the hole. Sixteen-tenths of a millimeter larger, thirty-two-tenths, and then sixty-four-tenths: it grew bigger exponentially each time, until toward the end when Roma was making huge leaps with each effort. And then the hole was wide enough. And Roma stepped through.

≈≈≈

I emerged on the other side. There was a narrow passageway. The ceiling was low, the walls off-white. At the end of passageway was a door. It was closed and light seeped under it.

I walked toward it.

Carved into the door, at eye level, was my name written in qubits. I turned the doorknob, pushed it open. I entered what looked like a little office, nothing fancy. On one wall was a whiteboard with black notes scribbled. There were two desks, two chairs, and two MacBooks. Seated at one of the chairs was the Troll. He wore blue jeans, sneakers, and a white T-shirt. He was big, even bigger than I'd remembered.

The Troll cleared his throat. I felt the presence of his charisma, like it was a living thing. He took a sip from a soda can, and then placed it down on the desk. He looked at me and without smiling said, "You finally made it."

"Yes." I felt like my entire life had led to this moment.

"Good. Are you ready to work? We've just gotten started."

Thank you for reading.
Please review this book. Reviews help others find New
Pulp Press and inspire us to keep providing these
marvelous tales.

If you would like to be put on our email list to receive
updates on new releases, contests, and promotions, please
go to NewPulpPress.com and sign up.

Acknowledgements

My continued gratitude to Rob Richardson, Al Riske, Greg Bardsley, and Anne Stewart for their support, willingness to read my work, and their honest and insightful feedback. I'm deeply appreciatative of Shirrel Rhoades and the fact that he saw something worthwhile in this book. Of course, my love and ongoing gratitude goes to Jennifer Leonard.

About the Author

Hunt for the Troll is Mark Richardson's debut novel. His short fiction has appeared in numerous literary and crime journals, including *Hobart, Fugue, Segue, Crime Factory, Switchback,* and *Prime Number Magazine.* He lives in Northern California with his wife and two children.

NewPulpPress.com